FROM GRUMPY TO FOREVER

Trickle Creek: The Lyons

Book 1

ELENA AITKEN

Trickle Creek

<u>The Lyons</u>
From Grumpy to Forever
More Than Words
Fake It 'Till We Fall
Best Friend Trap
Only For Tonight

<u>The Carlsons</u>
Never Let Me Go
If I Can't Have You
Always Be Mine
Because You Loved Me
Keep On Loving You

From Grumpy to Forever

I don't do love, forever, or marriage—but Avery Walker needs a husband, and I need the cash. A quick, convenient "I do," and we both get what we want. But with every lingering glance and late-night renovation, pretending this is just a business deal gets a hell of a lot harder.

Chapter One

Reid

THE ONLY THING worse than ripping out century-old hardwood floors from a heritage house was doing it for a privileged asshole and his plastic trophy wife who'd just moved to my quiet, small town with plans to "modernize and improve" things.

And there was no way I was going to do it.

To hell with the fat paycheck that would come with the job.

Never mind that the money these assholes were willing to pay me to destroy their beautiful house and turn it into a McMansion with no soul was enough to buy me a new set of woodworking tools.

And maybe even my own workshop, too.

"Not fucking worth it," I muttered, pissed at myself that I'd even considered taking the job in the first place.

I tugged my gloves off and shoved them in my back pocket before grabbing my toolbox.

"Off to get supplies?" The bottle blonde with tits almost as big as her head stopped me before I could make my escape. She wore skin-tight jeans and something that could barely be considered a bra the way she spilled out of it, with a silky plaid shirt tied around her waist. No doubt in an effort to look *small town.*

"Changed my mind," I told her. "I can't take the job."

"Sure you can." She wiggled herself closer and pulled her shoulders back to give me a better view of her store-bought assets.

"No." I turned away and headed for the door, almost sorry to leave this beautiful house, knowing that soon it would be a whitewashed, sterilized version of its former glory. "I can't."

I wasn't an idiot, and I also wasn't the only handyman in town. Someone else would take the job. Of that, I had no doubt. But it wouldn't be me.

"Stop!" the woman shrieked, when she finally figured out I wasn't playing. "Phillip! He's leaving!"

I had already loaded my toolbox in the back of my truck, when Phillip caught up to me. "Where do you think you're going?"

"I'm not taking the job."

"You already did."

"Then I quit." When I turned around, he was so close, I almost bumped into him. If he was trying for intimidation, it wouldn't work. He might have more money than me—by a lot—but I was at least half a foot taller, with a good fifty pounds of muscle on him. Not that I actually thought this man had ever used anything but his wallet to get what he wanted.

"You can't quit."

"Already did." I put my hand on the door handle. I was already done with this conversation. "I'm not going to be part of you destroying this gorgeous old house just so you can turn around and sell it to some other outsider for double market price. I won't be part of it."

"We're improving the property." Phillip obviously didn't like to be told no. His face turned a very unnatural shade of purple. "And this entire backwoods little town. You're an idiot if you don't want to—"

"What did you just call my town?" He cowered just the way I knew he would when I took a step toward him. "Call me whatever you want. But you don't fuck with my town, got it?"

The man nodded and swallowed hard before I stepped back and swung the truck door open. "Do yourself a favor, Phillip. Spend your money on your wife's next boob job and leave my town alone."

His bravado returned the moment I fired up the old truck. He was yelling something about me never working in this town again as I peeled away from the curb and the entitled asshole.

Okay, I might have gone a little too far with that last comment about his wife's tits, but I couldn't stop myself. It was people like Phillip and his plastic wife who would be the end of our town and everything that made it special.

It was bad enough with the ski resort and the new fancy golf course drawing in tourists both summer and winter, but now the city folk were starting to buy up properties. Things were changing in Trickle Creek, and I didn't like it.

I was still simmering in my shitty mood when I pulled up

in front of the hardware store. The last thing I should be doing was tool shopping with my bank account looking as anemic as it did, but it was the one thing that would make me feel better.

Well, maybe not the *one* thing. But the odds of me finding a woman willing to put up with my mood was even less likely than me walking out of the store with the new thickness planer I'd been eyeing.

"Reid." My twin brother, Grayson, greeted me the moment I stepped through the doors. He'd been more or less running the store for the last few years since Old Man Holbrook broke his hip. "What are you doing here? I thought you took that job over at—"

"I don't want to talk about it."

"Don't tell me you got fired again."

"Actually, I quit." I glared at him. "And I'll have you know, I didn't get fired from the job up at the Carlson condo units either."

"Oh, right." Gray didn't even bother to hide his smirk. "I suppose you quit that one, too. It had nothing to do with Asher telling you it wasn't okay to be rude to the guests?"

I didn't bother to answer him because he wasn't entirely wrong. Although it was more of a mutual understanding between Asher and me. Still, Grayson's comment pissed me off.

"Listen, Reid. I know you don't like it, but the tourists are here to stay." Grayson moved around the counter and started to walk down the aisle toward the plumbing fittings.

Against my better judgment, and my lack of interest in listening to a lecture, I followed him.

"And whether you see it or not, it's good for the town."

He wasn't wrong. A fact that pissed me off even more. The Carlson family had done a lot to build up the tourism industry in Trickle Creek, effectively saving the town from ruin after the old mine closed and so many jobs were lost.

But it didn't mean I had to like it.

"You know," Grayson looked at me while he reached into a box and started restocking a bin of parts, "maybe instead of fighting it, you should try embracing the change. You could do really well here if you stopped fighting with all your potential clients."

"But they're all such assholes."

Grayson shot me a look and leaned past me to greet the new customer the bells over the door just announced. "I'll be right with you."

He dropped the part he was holding back in the box and looked me in the eye. "You know the other perk of all the new faces in town?"

"What's that?"

Grayson wiggled his eyebrows and chuckled as he gestured with his head toward the front of the store. "A lot of those new faces are beautiful women."

Instinctively, I turned around. My gaze landed on the firm, round ass of Grayson's new customer, bent over looking at something on a bottom shelf. My long-dormant dick twitched to life. "Fuck me."

My brother laughed. Before he walked past me, he turned. "You know the best part, Reid?"

"What's that?"

"If they're new to town, they don't know what a grumpy asshole you are yet."

Chapter Two

Avery

THE HARDWARE STORE smelled like sawdust and paint, and I had absolutely no idea where to start. The small bag of tools I'd collected over the years of apartment living looked more and more pathetic by the second.

And more than a little inadequate for the project I'd just signed on for. I probably should have been even slightly more prepared, or at the very least, I should have considered that I'd need more than a hammer, screwdriver, and miniature measuring tape, all with pink and purple flowers on them.

Yes, flowers. The set was a gift from my best friend when I got my first apartment: *"In case you need to hang a picture or do a little home repair."*

I don't think Carrie had *renovate an entire rundown inn* in mind when she'd given it to me.

Just thinking of my best friend's shocked reaction when I

told her I was moving to Trickle Creek to take on the old project made me laugh as I scanned the aisles of the shop.

Row after row of tools and materials that I only barely recognized stretched out in front of me. I had no idea where to start.

Truthfully, I'd probably need one of everything. But for now, I needed whatever tool would help me actually get inside the old inn—and my new home.

"Can I help you find something?"

The voice startled me, and I jumped up from where I was bent over examining a bin full of work gloves.

"Sorry." The man chuckled. "I didn't mean to startle you."

"You didn't...I mean, you did." His easy smile and kind eyes put me at ease. "And yes, you can definitely help me find something. Everything, actually."

"Why don't we start with one thing and go from there." He held out his hand. "My name's Grayson Lyons. I run this shop. If I can't help you find what you need, I'll be able to find someone who can."

I shook his hand as my smile returned to my face. "That's exactly what I needed to hear today, Grayson. I'm Avery. I just moved to town and...well, like I said, I'm going to need *all* the things. I'm going to be fixing up the Tamarack Inn."

"You're going to be doing what?"

A deep voice responded from somewhere behind me, and I spun to see a man who looked just like Grayson, except with a frown that looked like it had taken up permanent residence on his face instead of Grayson's friendly grin.

His gaze landed on me and for a second, something

flickered deep in my gut—something that made my cheeks heat.

"Reid," Grayson said. "This is Avery." He made the introduction, but Reid didn't take his eyes off me. "Reid's my brother," he explained unnecessarily. "My much grumpier and far less handsome *twin* brother."

"We're identical," Reid grumbled, and I bit back a laugh.

"Except for that scowl on your face, brother."

Reid shook his head and ignored him when he asked, "Did you say you're fixing up the Tamarack Inn?"

"That's right," I said brightly, refusing to let his grumpiness intimidate me. "It's going to be gorgeous when I'm done."

"That's a big project." Reid crossed his thick arms over his chest. "You doing it on your own?"

"That's the plan." I shrugged. "Although I'm sure I'll need help with a few things. YouTube will only get me so far."

"YouTube?"

I thought Reid might choke.

Grayson only laughed and pulled my attention away from his brother. "I'm sure we'll be able to help you out, Avery."

Reid made a snorting sound I chose to ignore.

"Where should we begin?" Grayson asked.

"Well, I think we should probably start with getting me inside the inn." I held up my hands and shrugged. "I only have a key to the back door and I don't know if the lock is seized or what, but I can't get in."

Grayson chuckled. "Getting inside would be a good

place to start but it's hard to know what you need without actually seeing the situation myself."

I held my breath for a second, hoping maybe he'd suggest making the quick drive over to check it out.

"Reid?"

His brother had started to walk away toward the back of the store but stopped when Grayson said his name. He shook his head once before turning around. "What?"

"You have some time on your hands, don't you? I'm the only one working today, so I can't leave the shop. Why don't you go with Avery to see what the issue is?"

I could see it on his face—he was going to object. I couldn't let that happen. "Please," I said quickly. "I'd really appreciate it. I can pay you. I have enough—"

"Oh no." Grayson cut me off. "There's no need for that. We look out for our own in Trickle Creek."

The gratitude that washed over me was palpable. Even as a child, I'd felt like Trickle Creek was exactly where I belonged. And now…well, thanks to my grandparents' generosity, I was going to be able to live here. When the lawyer contacted me with the details of my grandfather's will, I'd been in shock that they'd left me the inn. A decision that was made years earlier. It was only just starting to sink in that they'd left it all to me.

Along with my husband. The husband I did not have.

But…that was a detail I was still trying to work out with the lawyer. For now, I needed to focus on the problem at hand.

"Thank you. I really appreciate your—"

"She's not one of our own," Reid grumbled. When I turned to look, his dark eyes were fixed on me with an unreadable expression. "If I had to bet, she's from the city."

"I am." I flashed him a bright grin. "Born and raised, in fact." I refused to be intimidated by this man. He didn't know it yet, but I wasn't easily deterred. As a pretty, petite blonde who always looked on the bright side, I'd spent my entire life being underestimated, particularly by rough and gruff macho men.

"But I used to visit Trickle Creek every summer and stay at the Tamarack Inn," I told the men. "I have a lot of fond memories of summers spent at the inn with my grandparents." A familiar twinge of sadness flashed through me the way it always did when I thought of them, but I pushed it down.

"Your grandparents used to bring you here?" Grayson asked. "For a holiday?"

"Oh no," I told him. "They owned the Tamarack Inn."

I turned to see the surprise on Reid's face. "Your grandparents were the Walkers?"

Again, the hurt in my chest twinged at the way he referred to them in the past tense, but I kept a smile on my face as I nodded. "And now I do."

"You own it?"

"I sure do," I told Reid. "So, I guess I'm one of your own after all." My use of finger quotes made Grayson laugh and slap his brother on the back.

"She's got you there. And Reid here is the best handyman in town, isn't that right, brother? And just so happens to be looking for work."

He gave his brother a sharp look before he dropped his head and grumbled something under his breath. After a moment, he finally looked up. "Okay," he said. "I'll see if I can help."

"Thank you." I clapped my hands together. "I'm parked right out—"

"I'll drive myself." With a shake of his head, Reid walked past us both, shooting his brother a dirty look on his way by. "I'll meet you there."

As soon as Reid was out of earshot, I turned to thank Grayson. "I really appreciate your help. It was nice to meet you."

"The pleasure was all mine, Avery." He laughed and shook his head a little. "And I have a feeling I'll be seeing a lot of you. Don't hesitate to ask for help if you need it. We'll do what we can."

"We?" I tipped my head.

"He's moody, but he's a good man," Grayson said. "You just have to look past the crunchy exterior to the gooey insides."

"Gooey, huh?" It was my turn to laugh. "I'll see about that."

"Actually," Grayson winked at me, "I have a feeling that you might."

Chapter Three

Reid

THE TAMARACK INN had seen better days.

It used to be a beautiful old building with robin's-egg blue siding and white shutters, and a wraparound porch where guests could gather in the evening and admire the perennial flower beds. It had a perfect location, just a few blocks off the pedestrian-only plaza that served as the hub of Trickle Creek with shops, cafes, and restaurants. The inn was once the only place for visitors to stay when they came to town.

When I was a boy, I used to think it was the biggest building I'd ever seen. With three floors and twelve rooms, it was hardly a skyscraper, but for Trickle Creek, it was a focal point to be sure.

At least, it had been. Before the condos were built up at the ski hill, drawing hundreds more tourists to town, but not to the inn with its old charm and personal touch.

Now, I couldn't help but feel a twinge of sadness to see the once beautiful gardens overgrown with weeds, the paint peeling and chipping off the siding, and the sagging porch.

I never knew them well, but the Walkers had always been friendly, and the pride they had for their inn had been apparent.

I vaguely remembered they had a granddaughter who was around when we were kids.

But I certainly didn't remember she was a very cute, way too fucking perky granddaughter.

While I sat there, assessing the dilapidated inn, Avery pulled in behind me. Of course, her car was a lemon-yellow Volkswagen. There were probably giant daisy decals on the —yup. Just as I suspected, when I stepped out of the truck, I saw the big flower stickers on the side of her car.

I shouldn't have been surprised.

"Did I keep you waiting?" She bounced from the car, her ponytail swinging and her breasts—

No. I had no business looking at her tits.

Even if her T-shirt was stretched tight over them, show-casing just how full and round and absolutely perfect they were.

"You didn't." With a growl, I shook my head and grabbed the toolbox from the back of my truck. "Let's get this over with."

She led the way up the porch, which gave me a nice view of her ass in her jeans. Just like her breasts, it was full and round and very fucking tempting.

"I can't tell you how much I appreciate this, Reid. I know there are going to be lots of challenges with the inn, but I guess I didn't expect the very first one to be getting in." Avery kept up a steady stream of chatter as we made our way to the back of the inn, and the troublesome door.

"Do you ever stop talking?"

Avery stopped walking so abruptly, that I tripped over myself to keep from crashing into her. She spun around to face me, the pretty smile still on her face. "I do, actually," she said. "But it's usually when I'm quiet that you need to worry."

"Worry?"

She winked at me and, with a flip of her ponytail, turned and kept walking.

I was going to kill Grayson for tricking me into helping this woman. Not only was she an outsider—and she was, no matter what anyone else said—she was infuriatingly upbeat. That might not be a completely negative trait for most people, but after the day I'd had, I'd much rather be alone with a cold beer than deal with this level of sunshine.

"This is the door." Avery waved her arm in the direction of the only door on the back side of the building. "It's the only key I was given. The rest are supposed to be inside. I don't know what's wrong, but the door just won't budge."

No shit it wouldn't open.

It didn't take a handyman to see that the door was painted shut and obviously hadn't been used in more years than the inn had been abandoned.

"Who gave you the key?"

"The lawyer." She held out a ring with one key on it. "Along with the paperwork telling me this place is mine."

"So your grandparents just left it to you, and you didn't know?"

"My grandfather passed away last month." It was the first time since I'd met her that her bright smile dimmed a little.

"I'm sorry," I said genuinely. "Mr. Walker was a good man."

Avery nodded curtly. "He was never the same after my grandma died," she said. "And when my parents moved him into the city, well…" She shrugged and squeezed her eyes shut for a second. "Anyway." When she opened her eyes again, some of the brightness had returned. "Turns out they decided when I was young that they wanted me to have it but never told anyone." She blew out a sigh. "But I couldn't be happier, and I'm going to do my best to bring it back to life." She flashed me that pretty smile that somehow had already started to grow on me. "Just as soon as I get in."

"Right." I took the key from her despite the fact I already knew there was no way it was going to open the door I was looking at. "You're sure it's not for the front door?"

She nodded.

"You tried?"

"Of course I tried it." Avery put her hands on her hips and her lips twisted into a frown, making me chuckle.

"Oh. You can smile."

"That's not a smile." I turned away and tried the key in the door. Even if it was made for the lock, there was no way it was going to open it. "This is a lot more than a seized lock. Do you want me to break it open?"

"Break it?"

"You do want to get in, don't you?"

"Well…I mean…"

15

"Yes or no."

It wouldn't be hard to crack the door off the frame. I reached down to my toolbox and grabbed my crowbar. "I can just break—"

"Wait!"

Avery

I grabbed Reid's arm moments before he could use his big iron bar to break open the door. It took me a minute to let go. Mostly because I was in shock at the size of the bicep beneath my hands.

Holy shit. This man was ripped.

When Reid lowered his arm and the tool, I had no choice but to release my hold on him.

"Okay." He turned around. "I thought you wanted to get in."

"I do, but..." I raised my arms and dropped them uselessly at my sides. "Can't we do it without destroying something? I mean, there's already so much for me to fix, I don't really want to add one more thing to the list. Plus, I don't really like the idea of being alone in here with a big gaping hole in the house."

I could see the gears turning in his head as he thought about it. For a moment, I was convinced he was going to pack up his tools and walk away from me and the inn completely. I couldn't let that happen. Not before I got inside.

Besides, I kind of liked him. Even if he was unbearably

grouchy, I was starting to think his brother might be right and there was a gooey center in there somewhere. And I did like a challenge.

Finally, Reid sighed with a shake of his head and dropped the bar. "Okay. Maybe I can find a window to jimmy open. Even if it breaks, it won't be as big a deal. Besides, you're probably going to have to replace most of them anyway."

Fresh hope surged through me. "Great."

Reid gave me a look. "It's not great yet. Let me find a window first."

Like a puppy dog, I trailed behind him as Reid circled the building, testing all the windows. Finally, he stopped at a side window that was one of the first he tested. "I think this is the best chance. It's loose." He jiggled it again, and I could see it move. "The locking mechanism probably needs to be replaced." He pulled a screwdriver from the tool belt that was slung low over his hips. "If I just…" He stuck the screwdriver in the space between the window and the base, and with a twist of his wrist, it popped open.

"Oh my God. You did it."

For the second time, there was the slightest trace of a grin on his lips. "Did you doubt me?"

"No." I couldn't help but laugh. "Well, maybe a little. But I'm so glad you got it. Thank you so much."

Clearly uncomfortable with the praise, Reid cleared his throat and looked down. "Yeah, it's nothing."

He turned to go, and once more, I stopped him with a hand on his arm. I let it linger a little longer, enjoying the feel of his strength under my touch. "Before you go…"

Reid looked at my hand on his arm as he turned around again, but he didn't pull away.

"Do you think you could give me a lift?"

Together, we both turned to the window that was just high enough off the ground that there was no way I was going to be able to scramble my way up on my own.

I flashed him another grin.

He shook his head and, with an exasperated sigh, said, "Of course."

Before I could brace myself, Reid's hands were on my hips. As if I weighed nothing, he lifted me until I was even with the window ledge and could try to scramble up.

There was no way around it—there was nothing glamorous about climbing into a window. I managed to get my knee up on the ledge before I slipped. My squeal died on my lips when Reid's hands caught me. The last thing I should have been thinking of was his big, strong hands on my ass, but how could I not? They fit perfectly, and I was almost disappointed when he gave me a shove through the window before releasing me.

Almost.

I landed with a thud on the dirty hardwood. The moment I looked up into what would have been a sitting room of the old inn, the only thing I was thinking about was that this was all mine.

"Wow." The word was barely more than a breath on my lips as I got to my feet and started to walk through the room, taking it all in.

The very first thing that struck me was how beautiful the old wooden floors and plaster walls with molding must have been in their prime. It wasn't something I would have noticed as a girl.

The second thought I had was just how much work it was going to be. I was definitely going to need help.

"Reid, I—"

He was already gone.

Chapter Four

Reid

"REID! WAIT UP."

I'd just fired up my old truck and put it in gear when Avery's voice reached me through my open window. When I turned, I saw her running down the path and across the overgrown front lawn toward me.

At least she got the front door open.

With a shake of my head, I put the truck in park.

"You weren't going to leave, were you?"

That's exactly what I was going to do. Avery seemed like a nice enough woman, if not a bit overly happy for my taste, but she was a city girl. And no matter how sexy she looked in that tight T-shirt and how well my hands had fit her round ass cheeks, *just right*, that was enough of a reason for me to keep my distance from her.

Even if my dick had other ideas.

"Places to go," I said. "Besides, you got in okay. I figured you'd want some time to check things out."

"Oh, I'll need some time all right." Her big blue eyes widened, and she sucked in a breath. "In fact, I think it's going to take me awhile to figure things out. But that's actually why I stopped you. Well, that and I wanted to thank you again. I don't know how I would have gotten in if you—"

"You would have figured it out." I forced myself to look over her head at the inn. If I didn't, my eyes were going to keep dipping down to the very inviting cleavage that my vantage point of the truck afforded me. "You seem like a very capable woman."

It was true. Even though the only tools she seemed to own were pink with flowers on them, Avery seemed a lot more competent than most of the city girls I ran into these days.

And a lot cuter, too.

Especially when she smiled at me like that.

"I'd like to think I'm not totally useless," she said. "But it doesn't take an expert to see that I'm going to need help with this." Her pretty smile faded a little. "I think in my head it was still the same place I remembered from when I was a kid, you know? I guess I didn't really expect..." She turned to look at her project.

I followed her gaze and saw the inn through her eyes. To say it was a fixer-upper would be giving it the benefit of the doubt.

It would have been a challenge for someone who knew what they were doing. For a DIY-er, it was going to be a project of monumental proportions.

"It is a big project." My eyes traveled over the peeling paint and the sagging porch. I remembered exactly how beautiful the inn had been once. More than once, I'd driven past and thought about what it would take to restore it to its former glory if only I had the capital. "It's a magnificent building," I said almost to myself. "A handyman's dream."

"Is it?" She spun around to face me, her eyes sparkling. "A handyman's dream?"

Her enthusiasm should have been my warning.

"It is," I answered honestly. "It's a heritage building and without inspecting it, I'd guess that it was built properly and has good bones. If I remember correctly, there were some quality plank floors and unique details throughout. With the right care, I have no doubt it'll be a rewarding project, for—"

"You."

My head snapped away from the inn to see Avery nodding. "No."

"Yes." Her hand reached out to squeeze my arm. Her touch was hot on my skin, sending sparks through my bloodstream directly to my dick that still hadn't received the message that this woman was off-limits.

"No." I pulled my arm back and instantly regretted it. "I'm not the man for this project."

"But why not?" Avery stepped back and wrapped her arms around her waist. "Your brother said you were the best handyman in town, and I need the best for this. The *inn* deserves the best. Besides, didn't he say you were looking for work?"

It was tempting. Working on a project of that size and quality would be amazing. Something I could really sink my teeth into. But... "No," I said again. "I won't be a part of the destruction of this town."

Avery took a sharp step back as if I'd slapped her. "The destruction...what are you talking about?"

"The last thing this town needs is more tourists coming in here and destroying everything that's special about Trickle Creek." My thoughts flashed back to my clients from earlier and their determination to strip every single piece of uniqueness and charm from their property. I'd be damned if I would be part of that very thing happening to the Tamarack Inn.

"Look." I put my hand on the gear shift. "I know your type, Avery. And I might not be able to prevent the destruction of this town, but I sure as hell am not going to be a part of it."

"Reid, I—"

"Find someone else," I said, and like the asshole I am, I put the truck in drive. "Good luck, Avery." And I drove away.

Chapter Five

Avery

"IT'S INCREDIBLE. I can't wait to see it in person."

The virtual tour over, I laughed and flipped the screen on my phone around so I could see my best friend, Carrie. "It's pretty great, isn't it?"

"It looks like a lot of work." Carrie pressed her lips together and shook her head.

Carrie and I had been best friends most of our lives. We'd been through pretty much everything together. But where I was an infallible optimist who could always see the bright side of every situation, Carrie was more of a realist. She'd tried to bring me back down to earth on more than one occasion in the past. But when it came to the inn, I refused to entertain any thoughts that weren't one hundred percent positive.

I couldn't afford to let any bit of negativity—or realism—in.

"I'm up for it." I took my cup of tea out to the front porch, which had very quickly been my favorite place in the few days I'd already been in town. Probably because from the vantage point of the old swing, with the building at my back and the street in front of me, I could pretend—at least for a few minutes—that I didn't have an overwhelming amount of work in front of me.

The swing creaked under my weight when I sat, but the rusty chain held. For now.

I added it to my mental list of things to fix.

"And I'm going to hire a handyman," I told Carrie once I was safely settled in the swing. "Reid Lyons is the best in town." It wasn't just his brother, Grayson, who'd told me that, either. I'd been asking around, and everyone had said the same thing.

"Is he cute?" Leave it to Carrie to need the details. "He is, isn't he? I can see it on your face."

It was true. Reid Lyons was *very* cute. And strong. And he made me feel things I hadn't felt in a very long time just by looking at me. But he was also the grouchiest man I'd ever met, completely unreasonable, and—probably most notable—he didn't seem to like me at all.

"Oh my God, Avery. You are totally living in a Hallmark movie."

"A what?"

"You are. You've moved to a small mountain town to fix up the old inn you inherited and you're going to fall in love with the sexy local handyman." She laughed. "It's just like every single holiday movie ever."

"Except it's not Christmas time."

"Details, details." Carrie waved her hand.

And then there was the other, not-so-small detail that I still hadn't fully resolved about the fact that my grandparents' will had clearly stated I needed to be married in order to inherit the inn and the healthy savings account they'd left me to fix it up.

"You forget that I still haven't figured out the rest of my situation." I bit my bottom lip and blew out a breath.

"I'm telling you, Avery. Just grab a guy off the street and make him a deal. You're a total catch, and any man would be more than happy to be your husband."

"Except for one." I hated the way my stomach still dropped six months later whenever I was reminded of Porter.

"He's a fucking idiot," Carrie said without missing a beat. "And he did you a favor by knocking up that—"

"I don't want to talk about it."

I didn't. Mostly because there was nothing to talk about. Porter and I had been together just over a year, and I was sure we were going to be married. It wasn't just me, either. Porter loved to talk about the big wedding we were going to have, with all our family and friends. I could see now that for him, the wedding would have been more to show off and a lot less about *us* and our relationship. But it hadn't stopped me from starting to daydream about standing at the altar, pledging my life and love to my husband.

I just had the wrong man.

Ironically, if I hadn't discovered that Porter had been sleeping with his intern, I probably would have that husband I needed right now. Of course, if she hadn't gotten pregnant, I would have been married to an adulterer. So, be thankful for small blessings, I guess.

"Well, either way, I meant what I said." Carrie shook her head. "All you need to do is go outside and wave your left hand in the air, and you'll snag a husband."

"You do realize how crazy that sounds, right?"

"Hell, I'll marry you right now." Carrie looked straight into the camera.

It was my turn to laugh. "Is that a proposal?"

"You know it is." She was completely serious. "But I'm not wearing white."

"Oh, I love you, Carrie," I said between giggles. "But the will clearly stated *husband*, so I'm pretty sure it's a no-go. You know how much I appreciate it, though."

"Anything for you." She blew me a kiss. "Look, I can't wait to see the inn and this sexy handyman you're going to fall in love with and marry. Or marry and then fall in love with." She waved her hand. "Whatever order you need to do things. But I've gotta run. Talk soon, okay?"

"Of course."

"Love you, bye." The screen went blank.

"A Hallmark movie, huh?" I tucked my phone beneath me, took a sip of my tea, and pushed the swing a little so my feet slid over the floorboards. The situation did have all the makings for one of the over-the-top sappy movies I loved to binge with a bucket of popcorn. Except for one little detail.

This was real life. Not a movie.

With a sigh, I dropped my head back and blew out a breath. I couldn't let myself worry about the whole *husband* thing. Not until it was something to actually worry about.

And with any luck, the lawyers would find a loophole that rendered that part of the will null and void.

For now, I needed to focus on the task at hand.

Getting this place fixed up.

It had taken me a few days to conclude, but I'd officially reached it. YouTube videos and internet searches were only going to get me so far when it came to the repairs the inn needed.

Despite my best efforts, I'd been unable to get Reid to accept the job. Of course, it would help if I could actually talk to him, but I hadn't been very successful in my efforts to track him down up until now.

And even if I could find Reid, I wasn't overly confident that I'd be able to convince him of anything. He was pretty adamantly against helping me with the inn. Which was completely ridiculous. No matter what he might think, I was not an outsider who was going to singlehandedly destroy his town.

Okay, I might be an outsider. But I certainly had no plans to destroy Trickle Creek.

I'd only been back in town for a few days and already I remembered exactly why I loved it here so much when I was younger.

Everything was so much quieter and calmer. With the mountains surrounding me in every direction, I felt a sense of peace that I could never achieve in the city. No matter how many yoga classes or meditation sessions I attended.

It was like some part of me was able to unplug and disconnect so that I could reconnect to a different part of myself. A calmer, more connected part.

With a sigh, I took another sip of my tea and let my feet slide over the floorboards again.

I was going to need help and if Reid wasn't willing to take the job, I was just going to have to find the second-best handyman in Trickle Creek.

And possibly—a husband.

The sooner the better.

Chapter Six

Reid

MY WORKSHOP SPACE was cramped and crowded with the tools I'd acquired over the years. My wish list for tools was much, much longer than what I actually had on hand.

The problem was quality tools cost money. Money I didn't have.

You'd have plenty of money if you stopped getting fired.

I could hear my twin brother's voice echoing in my head. But Grayson didn't think about things the way I did. He never had.

He didn't see the way the newcomers were ruining our town. To him, every new person moving to Trickle Creek was a new customer. It wasn't that he didn't care about the way things were changing; it just didn't bother him the way it did me.

The last thing I wanted was for Trickle Creek to turn into another soulless tourist town. It had already happened to so many of the small towns that were a little closer to the city. The city folk moved in and took over, as if it were their own personal playground to do with what they liked.

Sure, some of them were decent people who were just looking for an escape from the city and respected the small-town life. But far too many of them wanted all the conveniences of the city, only in the mountains.

They threw their money around, changing things just enough to drive out the small mom-and-pop shops, bringing in the drive-thrus and corporate, soulless stores that transformed the unique, character-filled town into a mini version of the city.

I'd be damned if I was going to let that happen to Trickle Creek.

Things had already changed too much. The Carlson family was beloved in town for boosting tourism when the mines shut down and hundreds of people lost their jobs. Under Michael Carlson's leadership, a ski resort and golf course were built, along with a large lodge and condos that brought a lot of attention to our little town. And with that attention came the tourists. And the money.

Truthfully, the changes did save the town, but now things were swinging too far. There had to be a compromise of some sort. Couldn't it be possible to have tourism while still preserving everything that made Trickle Creek special?

I wished I had the answers. But I didn't, so I turned my attention back to the project at hand. With my hands on my hips, I took a step back to assess the stack of wood I had.

Or, more specifically, I *tried* to take a step back before tripping over a stack of boxes my brother had piled up.

With a grumble, I only barely caught myself before falling on my ass.

The shed was too small to be a proper workshop. Especially when I had to share it with my brother Ethan and his brewery equipment. And I did have to share, because technically the shed I used as my workshop sat on his land and belonged to him.

A small detail that had never been a problem when Ethan and his daughter Quinn were living in the city. Ethan had given me free rent in his place and use of the shed as long as I took care of the property. But now, since the divorce was finalized, Ethan and Quinn were moving back to town.

Not only was I going to have to find a new place to live, I needed a real workshop space. The tiny shed was okay for small projects, but not the bigger furniture pieces I wanted to focus on.

And I had my eye on just the right spot on the edge of town that had just posted for sale. It was a great location, and there was even a little room that would be ideal as a showroom for completed pieces to prospective buyers.

It was perfect.

Except for the price tag.

Which meant that, like it or not, I was going to need to find some secure source of employment.

Avery's cute blonde head popped into my mind.

Working at the inn would be a big job. No doubt it would pay well. And there was the added benefit of working closely with Avery.

Just thinking of the overly optimistic and undeniably sexy woman made me shake my head. Yes, the woman could fill out a T-shirt, and the memory of the way her ass had fit perfectly in my hands when I boosted her into the window had given me something to think about every night while I lay alone in my bed. But her eternal optimism and over-the-top energy would drive me crazy if I worked for her.

Never mind the fact that it was never a good idea to sleep with your boss, or *want* to sleep with your boss.

And all of that was a big *if* anyway, considering I'd been a first-class asshole to her the other day.

No. Working on the inn was off the table. I was going to hustle for work the old-fashioned way.

"Fuck." Out of options, I tossed my gloves on the workbench, dusted off my hands, and headed out of the shed and into town. There was no way around it—I needed to find work.

Chapter Seven

Avery

THE DARK ROAST in front of me was hot and strong and, without a doubt, the best coffee I'd had since arriving in Trickle Creek. On the barista's advice, I also decided to treat myself to a freshly baked peanut butter cookie. And I was glad I had.

The blast of sugar and caffeine was the only thing getting me through the meeting with Danny Davis of Davis Done Right. Everything about this man gave me cringy vibes. He'd just spent the last twenty minutes talking over me and blowing off any of my questions and concerns about the renovations on the inn.

He either couldn't remember my name, or flat out refused to use it. But if he called me *darling* or *honey* one more time, I couldn't be held responsible for my actions.

The problem was, after asking around, Danny Davis was the only other name that came up as a reliable handyman.

After Reid Lyons, of course.

But he was still proving to be elusive and I couldn't wait around forever. I needed to get moving on my renovations. I was out of options.

Which was the only reason I hadn't already gotten up and left the table at the Bean Bag. Well, that and the delicious snack. Next time I was ordering to go.

"I can get started on this right away, honey. We'll be working pretty close—"

"It's Avery." I'd lost track of how many times I'd corrected him. "And I still have a few more people to talk to. So—"

"There's no one else, darling."

Danny was confident; I'd give him that. And after glancing through his portfolio of work, there weren't any major red flags. Except for the one, giant one currently waving over his head.

Unable to meet his gaze, I lifted the mug to my mouth and took a long, slow sip of coffee.

Working with Danny would be a challenge, and it would be far less enjoyable than...well, working with almost anyone else. But what were my other options?

"Danny, I need to think about—"

"Tell ya what, honey. I need to pop out for a minute and make a call." He stood up from the tiny table and loomed over it, tapping a big, meaty finger on the plans I'd brought with me. "Give it some thought and once you come to the right decision, I'll be back to make it official."

Somehow, I managed to force a smile. It wasn't often that someone made me feel so icky just by being in their presence, but Danny Davis had managed it in less than a half hour.

The smile—as fake as it was—fell off my face the moment Danny turned and walked away. I dropped my head and inhaled deeply before looking up.

Okay, Avery. Think.

My gaze landed on the plans I'd sketched out and the notes I'd made for the inn.

I could visualize it in my mind. The freshly painted blue siding with crisp, white trim. The garden beds once more free of weeds and full of blooms in the summer. Inside, the floors would be polished and gleaming the way they once were. A vase of fresh flowers would greet guests at the check-in desk before they climbed the big, open staircase to their freshly painted rooms.

Never mind everything that needed to be done behind the scenes. The plumbing, the kitchen... *Maybe I'd bitten off more than I could handle?*

It was the first time I'd allowed even the slightest bit of doubt to creep in, and almost as soon as I did, I pushed it out of my mind. I couldn't afford to let even the slightest negative thought in. As soon as I did...well, I couldn't go there.

The tinkle of the cafe door caught my attention. My head shot up, expecting to see Danny Davis returning already.

My heart leapt into my throat when I saw it wasn't Danny at all, but instead, Trickle Creek's number-one handyman who stood at the bulletin board by the entrance.

I watched while he scanned the selection of notices pinned there before shaking his head and pinning up his own paper, directly over the same flyer I'd looked at for Davis Done Right.

From where I was sitting, I couldn't make out the words on Reid's flyer, but I could see the image of a hammer.

He was advertising his handyman services? After turning down *my* job?

"Interesting." The word came out of my mouth before I could stop it.

Reid turned at the sound of my voice. The moment his eyes landed on me, his expression changed. His lips dipped down from a sullen smirk to a full-on frown. But his eyes sparked. "You're still here."

It wasn't a question.

"I never planned on going anywhere," I fired back. With my head, I gestured to the pinboard and the notice he'd just posted. "So it's just my job you don't want."

Reid glanced behind him before crossing the short distance to my table. His gaze dropped to the papers spread out in front of me. "These your plans?"

"They're a start." I shrugged. "Mostly just lists and ideas."

"Huh." Without asking, he slid the papers around, scanning the information.

"Huh? What does that mean?"

Finally, he looked up. His dark-brown eyes stared at me with such intensity, that my stomach clenched.

"It's ambitious is all."

"I can handle it." I put a smile on my face and tossed my hair over my shoulder. "Besides, I'm not going to be doing it alone."

His eyes darkened. "What do you mean? You're not doing it alone?"

It was the last thing I wanted, especially now that I had

Reid Lyons standing in front of me, but before I could stop myself, I told him, "I was just talking to Danny Davis."

Reid's nostrils flared.

"I'm going to hire him to—"

"To hell you are."

Reid

The words came out much stronger than I intended, and I regretted them the moment I saw Avery flinch. Her smile faltered, but her eyes flashed.

"Excuse me?" She straightened her shoulders and tilted her chin up. "Last I checked, you didn't have a say in who I hired to help me."

She wasn't wrong. I had absolutely no say. But I'd be dammed if I let Danny Davis anywhere near her. He was a sleazy son of a bitch who had no sense of ethics, morals, or a job well done.

Not only would Avery be wasting her money on a spit-and-polish cover-up job, but she'd be subjected to his demeaning harassment. And if he laid a hand on her— there was no fucking way.

"Don't hire him." I crossed my arms over my chest and stared down at her. "You'll regret it."

"Is that right?" She stood and crossed her arms, too. She was a good foot shorter than me but challenge sparked in her eyes, and I knew I was going to have a brand-new image of her occupying my thoughts at night.

"I don't suppose you'd care to give me a good reason I shouldn't hire him?" She fired the question at me. "I mean, if you can bring yourself to speak to an outsider like me, that is."

Fuck.

I regretted every single shitty thing I'd ever said to her. Especially if it had driven her to hire the likes of Danny Davis.

"Because he's not as good as me."

She laughed. She actually laughed. But there was no humor in it as she threw her head and chuckled before once more looking me in the eye. "You rejected me, remember?"

Oh, I remembered.

"And while I'm sure you think so highly of yourself to think that you're the best in town," she continued with a feisty side I hadn't seen in her the other day, "you're not the *only* guy in town. I have a job that needs to be done. And I *will* be hiring someone to do it. Whether you like it or not."

I didn't like it. Not one little bit. Not if it was Danny Davis she hired.

No. Scratch that.

I wouldn't like it if she hired anyone but me, and I damn well knew it. There was no way I was going to be able to sit by and watch anyone working closely with Avery day after day. I couldn't explain it. It didn't make any sense, and I certainly didn't have any right to feel protective over this woman. But I did.

And I'd be dammed if I let Danny anywhere near her.

"Hey, Lyons. Don't tell me you're bidding on this job, too?"

Unexplainable rage filled me at the sound of his voice. Somehow, I managed to control myself as I turned to see Danny. He held his hand out in greeting. I didn't move, keeping my hands stuffed under my arms still crossed over my chest.

"Davis." I nodded my greeting instead.

If he was deterred, he didn't show it. Instead, the sleazy asshole moved around the table until he stood next to Avery.

"I'm not bidding on this job," I told him.

"That's good to hear." While I watched, Danny put an arm around Avery's shoulders and pulled her into him.

I didn't miss the way she flinched before pasting that bright smile back on her pretty face.

My nostrils flared, and my fingers clenched into fists. I knew how I wanted to handle the situation, the way I always wanted to handle the situation when it came to this asshole, but that wasn't an option. Not with Avery standing right there.

Instead, I looked him right in the eyes and told him, "I'm not bidding on the job. Because I've already accepted it." I watched Avery closely as I spoke. Her eyes darted to mine, and the relief I saw there was clear and told me everything I needed to know.

She slipped to the side, ducked out from under Danny's arm and shifted just the tiniest bit toward me.

"What?" Danny looked between Avery and me. "Is that true? I thought we had something—"

"Sorry, Danny." To her credit, Avery actually did a pretty good job looking apologetic, despite the relief underlying her words. "I offered the job to Reid earlier and he just formally accepted." She looked up at me with a wicked grin. "He starts tomorrow."

Chapter Eight

Reid

"WAIT." My brother Ethan held the coffeepot aloft and stared at me. "You have a job? Seriously?"

"Don't look so surprised." I reached past him to grab a mug from the cupboard. "Rumor has it I'm Trickle Creek's best handyman."

Ethan laughed and thankfully filled my cup before returning the pot to the machine.

"What? You don't think so?" I leaned against the cupboard and glared at him.

"Oh no." My brother shook his head with a grin. "I don't doubt that you're the best. But you're also the grumpiest. And the way I heard it is that you can't keep your mouth shut long enough to keep a job these days."

"Grayson?"

Ethan nodded and took a sip of his coffee.

"He doesn't know what the hell he's talking about." I shook my head and muttered a string of expletives under my breath. The last thing I needed was my own twin brother running his mouth about my attitude on the job.

Even if it was true.

"I don't know," Ethan said. "He mentioned the other day about this huge opportunity you had to fix up the Tamarack Inn."

I lifted my eyebrows and waited to see what else my twin had to say about me.

"To hear Grayson tell it, the Walkers' granddaughter came in looking for a little help and you turned it down. He also mentioned she's very pretty."

"Did he?" I exhaled slowly, counting to ten under my breath.

"He sure did." Ethan wiggled his eyebrows.

I had to fight back the urge to say something I would definitely regret. After all, I was still living in his house.

"Too bad, though," he continued. "Gray said you were a total dick to her, and she hired Danny Davis instead."

I choked on my coffee. "Grayson needs to learn to keep his mouth shut or get the facts straight," I said when I'd recovered. "He doesn't have a fucking clue what he's talking about."

"She's not cute?"

"No," I said. "That part he got right. Avery's very fucking pretty." There was zero point in arguing that fact. Ethan had two eyes in his head, and in a town the size of Trickle Creek, it was only a matter of time before he met Avery himself.

A surge of jealousy and protectiveness I had no right to filled me. "Which means, you need to stay away from her." I shot him a glare over the rim of my cup.

My brother only laughed. "Right, because as a single dad of a hormonal pre-teen daughter, you think I have any interest in getting involved with another woman?" He shook his head. "She's all yours."

"She's not mine at all." I set my cup down and grabbed a granola bar from the box on the counter to serve as my breakfast. "But she is my boss," I added. "Your source got that piece of information wrong."

"No shit?"

I nodded. "There's no way I'd let Danny fuckin' Davis anywhere near that beautiful old inn."

"Or the pretty young inn owner, eh?"

I spun around and snarled at my brother, who only laughed harder.

"Whatever. I'm just glad you're working. Maybe you'll be able to get your own place."

I didn't miss the way his voice changed. "You kicking me out, brother?"

"Not yet."

"But soon."

"You know we love having you."

It was my turn to laugh.

"We do," he said. "Especially Quinn. And it's nice to have an extra set of hands to help with her."

My niece *was* a hormonal pre-teen, but she was the best thing that had happened to our family in a long time. And definitely, the very best thing to ever come out of my big brother's ill-fated marriage.

"Hey." I waved off his explanations. "It's not a big deal. It's time for me to get my space anyway. And a bigger workshop. I noticed some boxes moving in."

Ethan's face lit up. "My supplies are starting to arrive. I'm hoping to get something going in a few days and pretty soon I'll have a few brews to sample."

It was hard not to get excited about my brother's vision for a local brewery, especially when you saw the way it lit him up. Ethan deserved it after everything he'd been through with his ex.

"I can't wait, brother." I poured the rest of my coffee into a go-cup and stuck my phone in my pocket. "I better get going."

"Don't want to be late for the boss lady on the first day," Ethan said. "Especially if she's as cute as I hear."

"Uh-huh."

His laughter followed me down the hall before he called after me. "Don't forget you promised to meet Quinn for an ice cream this afternoon."

"You know I won't." I threw up an arm in a wave. "See ya later."

It was a short drive to the Tamarack Inn and not nearly long enough to get my brother's comments about Avery out of my head. I was going to have to pay my twin brother a visit later to make sure he kept his mouth shut about shit he knew nothing about.

And Grayson certainly didn't know anything about Avery or how I may or may not feel about her.

Did he?

Having an identical twin brother had its advantages, but it also had more than its fair share of disadvantages, too. And this was a perfect example of the latter.

Ultimately, it didn't matter what I thought about Avery. She was about to be my boss. Even if I couldn't quite figure out how that had happened either.

I'd replayed the whole scene in the Bean Bag over and over in my mind. If it had been anyone but Avery, I would have been positive that I'd been set up.

But Avery didn't seem like the devious type. Not even a little. She was far too *good.*

Far too good for me, that was for sure.

But I wasn't going to date her, I reminded myself as I pulled up in front of the inn and saw her petite form dressed in jean shorts, a bright-blue T-shirt, and a ball cap with her blonde ponytail sticking out the back.

She was bent over in the garden, tugging on a dead shrub, her perfectly round ass up in the air.

I swallowed hard and scrubbed a hand over my face.

No. I wasn't going to date her.

I was going to work for her.

That was it.

Chapter Nine

Avery

THE GARDEN WAS COMPLETELY out of control. Maybe clearing it out wasn't the highest thing on the very long list of things I needed to handle, but it was something I could do that would make a difference right away.

At least that had been my expectation when I started tugging on the old shrub. It proved more stubborn than I'd expected.

"Come on, you stupid thing." I gave it one last tug, putting my entire body weight behind it. At the same moment the roots started to give, I realized I was going to go over with it and go down hard on my backside.

"Whoa." A pair of strong, capable hands—that I'd felt once before—settled on my ass. "Careful."

I twisted around to see my savior. "Thank you."

He nodded and waited for a beat before setting me up on my feet and stepping back. "That's what I'm here for, right?"

"To catch me when I fall?" I tugged the gloves from my hands and dusted them off on my jean shorts. "I hope you're here for a lot more than that. After all, that's why I'm paying you the big bucks, right?"

He cocked his head, and I couldn't help the shot of desire that raced through me when he pinned me with those dark, mysterious eyes of his. "What *are* you paying me? We never really discussed details."

It was true. We hadn't discussed much of anything. Once he agreed to take the job, I was so relieved, I didn't stop to figure out any of the logistics. I didn't want to give him any reason to change his mind. "Come have a coffee and we can discuss the details before we get started."

He nodded, and I led him up the steps to the porch. Reid waited outside while I fetched two cups of coffee from the kitchen along with a pad of paper where I'd jotted down some numbers after a bit of research into the average prices of handyman services.

"Here." I handed him a mug and pointed to one of the old chairs against the wall. "You can sit there. I just love this swing."

Reid assessed the chair and shook his head. "I think I'll stand. Those chairs look like they've seen better days."

"They're on the list." I held up the pad of paper. "Along with almost everything else." My swing creaked and protested when I settled myself onto the bench.

Reid's eyebrows shot up, his eyes wide. "You're not going to sit on that?"

"It's my very favorite place to—"

This time, he couldn't move fast enough to catch me from the crash as the rusted old chain gave away and I, along with the swing, tumbled to the floorboards in a coffee-stained heap.

"Oh shit." Reid was at my side in an instant. "Are you okay?"

Before I could protest, he had a hand under my elbow and lifted me easily to my feet. His hand lingered on my elbow, holding me in place while I recovered from the upset.

"Looks like we should add fixing the swing to the list of things that need repair."

Unexpected, hot tears burned in my eyes. I blinked hard and looked down at my empty coffee cup. There was no way I was going to let myself cry. Not over a broken swing, of all things. Even if it was my favorite part of the house.

But it wasn't about the swing at all. It was just one more thing in a very long, and growing list of things that were starting to feel out of my control.

"It's okay, Avery."

Reid's hand was still on my elbow. It was the only thing keeping me from losing it altogether.

"I can fix this. No—"

"It's fine." I pasted a smile to my face and pushed the unexpected and unwelcome emotion down. "I think it just startled me. Don't worry about it."

I took a step back, and Reid's hand fell away. His eyes were dark with concern, but thankfully, he didn't push the issue because I had no idea how I would explain that the real reason I was on edge was that I'd received a message from the lawyer earlier to schedule a meeting to discuss what I was now referring to as *the husband clause*.

No, it was definitely best that I kept that detail to myself.

I didn't need to scare him off now that I'd finally gotten him to agree to the job.

Especially because if I couldn't figure out a solution to *the husband clause*, there would be no job at all. No inn. No money. No handyman needed.

It took me a few more moments to recover, but when I finally pulled myself together, we moved to the much safer —although not by much—porch steps to finish up the discussion of our working arrangement.

Reid's proposal was fair, and I agreed to it immediately, including a small retainer to get started. "I have to go over to the plaza later this afternoon for a meeting," I told him. "If you can wait a few hours, I can grab you some cash then. I'm good for it."

His lazy smile did something to my insides that was more than a little distracting. "That'll be fine." He reached for the notebook in my hand. "If it's okay with you, I'll spend some time going through the house and the list you have here so we can triage the biggest jobs and come up with a plan that makes the most sense so we don't waste time and money."

The amount of relief I felt knowing I was in competent hands with Reid almost made me want to cry again. Instead, I handed him the notepad.

"I'll leave you to it then." I stood up and dusted off my shorts. "I should be done with my meeting around two if you want to meet up and go over things then?" At least I hoped we'd be going over the details after the meeting.

There was still a chance that the lawyer couldn't find a loophole and I'd have to pivot my entire strategy. Or scrap it altogether, considering I didn't have a husband. But I was nothing if not an eternal optimist. It would all work out.

It had to.

"How about meeting at the Sugar Shack? They have the best ice cream in town." Reid was already down the steps when he turned.

What was it about the way he looked at me that felt *different?* It was probably just the stress I was under that had me seeing and feeling things that weren't there. Even if they might be there…

Getting involved with the man I'd just hired was not a good idea.

"It's a date then."

The words were out of my mouth before I realized how they would sound. My face heated, a blush that turned into a blaze when Reid said, "I wish it was. But I don't date people I work for."

"Oh. Right," I stammered, my face completely on fire with embarrassment. "I didn't mean it like…that's not what I—"

Reid saved me from digging myself in even deeper with a wink and what I was coming to think was a very rare grin. "See you this afternoon, boss lady."

Chapter Ten

Reid

"DAD SAYS you're going to live in the backyard forever."

The spoonful of mint chocolate chip hovered in the air as I assessed my niece from across the table. We had our usual table at the back of the shop, by the window where we could people-watch everyone in the plaza.

In the few short months since my brother had moved his daughter back to Trickle Creek, I'd made it a point to spend quality time with her to make up for all the years they'd been in the city and we only got to see them on holidays and the occasional long weekend.

If someone told me six months ago that I'd be looking forward to my regular ice cream dates with a twelve-year-old girl, I would have thought them insane. But truthfully, Quinn was a sharp, witty kid who had no problem saying it like it was, and I enjoyed her company more than most adults.

"He said that, did he?"

"Sure did." Quinn took a bite of her scoop, and I winced. "How do you do that?"

She shrugged. "Young teeth."

"You're saying I'm old?" I dipped my spoon back in for another bite.

"You're ancient." She laughed before taking another big bite of her ice cream. "So, are you? Going to live in the backyard forever?"

"For one," I pointed my spoon at her, "I don't live in the backyard. My shop is in the backyard. I have a room in the house, and you know it." Quinn shrugged, so I continued. "And two…no. I'm not. In fact, I just accepted a big job that pays quite well."

The work at the inn did pay pretty well, but it was the amount of work that Avery had in front of her that meant a decent and steady paycheck for the next little bit. It would definitely be enough to get my own place plus the workshop I'd already called the real estate agent about. The retainer Avery was going to give me this afternoon was just enough for the down payment. It would leave me short for a bit, but that was a temporary issue. The risk was worth it.

At least, it would be.

"You got a job?"

"You look surprised." I tried not to laugh. "I do work, you know."

"Dad says you're wasting your potential because of your misguided morals."

I put my spoon down and stared at my niece, finding it hard to believe that Ethan would have such a conversation with his twelve-year-old. "Is that right?"

She nodded and licked the drips off the bottom of her cone. "Yup. And Uncle Gray said that what you really need is a good woman to sort you out."

Ahh. That made a lot more sense. My niece had perfected the art of eavesdropping on all kinds of conversations when you thought she had her earbuds in, watching whatever garbage was on her phone. I made a note to mention to Ethan that he might want to use a little more discretion in the future when he was gossiping about me. Or anyone else, for that matter. Or, better yet, he could learn to keep his fucking mouth shut altogether.

But for the time being, I was going to use my brother's lack of discretion to my advantage.

"What else did they say?"

Quinn grinned and leaned across the table conspiratorially. "My dad said it was doubtful you would ever find a woman who'd put up with your grumpy ass."

"Hey."

"I didn't say it." She shrugged. "Dad did."

"Don't say ass." I pointed my spoon at her.

She rolled her eyes in response before continuing. "But Uncle Gray said that the right woman would be able to put a smile on your face."

He wasn't wrong. It had been way too long since any woman had put a smile on my face. Still, my twelve-year-old niece shouldn't be privy to any conversation that had the potential to quickly become R-rated. I was definitely going to have to talk to my brothers about discretion.

"She's new." Quinn pointed over my shoulder. "Doesn't look like a tourist, though. Too sad."

"Sad?" Curious, I spun in my seat to see who Quinn was pointing at.

Avery.

She'd traded her coffee-stained T-shirt and sinfully short cutoff shorts for a pretty blue wrap dress and strappy sandals. She looked gorgeous.

But Quinn was right. She also looked sad.

In the brief time I'd known Avery, she'd never once looked sad. Quite the opposite. She was the happiest, smiliest person I'd ever met.

With the exception of earlier when I could have sworn she was about to cry when her swing fell down. But I'd chalked that up to the shock of falling on her ass.

But this…

"She's really pretty." Quinn dove into our game of people-watching, completely unaware that the woman we were currently watching was on her way to meet us for an ice cream.

"She is," I agreed.

"I bet if she smiled, she'd be gorgeous."

"She is."

"You mean she *would* be."

I turned in my chair to see Quinn giving me a strange look. "No," I said. "She is gorgeous when she smiles. Her name is Avery. And she's my new boss. She's meeting us here."

Quinn's mouth fell open dramatically. "*She's* your boss?"

"She is." I grabbed a paper napkin and wiped my face before standing. "So be on your best behavior, okay?"

"Uncle Reid," Quinn leaned back in her chair, "I'm *always* on my best behavior."

I shot her a look at the same time the bells over the door chimed. I turned to greet Avery, who, just as I'd told my niece, was gorgeous with her bright smile on her face.

Even if it didn't reach her eyes this time.

Avery

"You're right, Uncle Reid. She is gorgeous."

The girl Reid had just introduced as his niece flashed a mischievous grin at her uncle. I couldn't help but laugh. Especially when Reid tripped all over his words.

"That's not really what I said. Or how it was said. But…"

He looked up and met my eyes, causing me to laugh again. It felt good after the meeting I'd just walked out of.

"She is gorgeous," he finished with a smile and a shrug. "Sorry about that."

"Oh," I shook my head, "please don't apologize for paying me a compliment." I winked at Quinn. "A woman never gets tired of hearing them. Do we, Quinn?"

She shook her head and licked her blue ice cream. "Nope. We women like to hear how pretty we are."

"Okay, okay." Reid tried to change the subject. "Avery, can I get you an ice cream? It's the best in town."

"Or anywhere," Quinn added.

"It's true. Craig Carlson started this shop a few years back, and it truly is the best."

What I really wanted was a glass of wine, or something stronger. Maybe a whiskey would be better suited considering the meeting I'd just come out of and the news I was going to have to deliver to Reid. The lawyer hadn't been able to find a loophole. Which meant I was about to lose the inn.

Keeping the smile on my face all of a sudden felt impossible. I dropped my gaze to the black and white tile floor for a moment in an effort to regain my composure.

"Hey."

Reid's hand on my bare arm was almost as good as the hug I really needed. I looked up into his concerned eyes.

"Not only is his ice cream the best, but it's pretty much known as fact to make any day better. Isn't that right, Quinn?"

"It's true," the girl said earnestly. "When I first moved here, I was having a bad day, missing my friends back home, and Uncle Reid brought me for ice cream."

The idea of the grumpy, growly Reid doing something so sweet made me melt a little. "He did?" I focused on the girl, which was for the best because Reid was still touching my arm and it was causing all kinds of sensations to race through me, which was only making me even more twisted up inside.

"Yup," she said matter-of-factly. "And now, every time I have ice cream with him, it's a good day."

Just like that, the smile came back naturally to my face. I looked at Reid, who shrugged.

"What can I say? It's powerful ice cream."

Something told me it had nothing to do with the ice cream.

"What do you say?" he pushed. "You seem like you might be a maple walnut kind of woman?"

"Maple walnut?" I pretended to be offended. "I'm a chocolate girl. The more the better."

Reid slid his hand off my arm. "I'll be right back."

A few minutes later, I was almost convinced that it was magical ice cream. The double chocolate fudge Reid handed me was groan-worthy delicious. But it was the banter between Reid and his niece that I had to credit for helping me forget my troubles. It seemed the grumpy handyman had met his match in a twelve-year-old girl.

"My uncle says you're his new boss." Quinn shifted the conversation to me, and just like that, I lost my appetite.

I pushed the cup of ice cream away. "I…well…I…"

"Actually, Quinn. Avery and I are going to go over the final details this afternoon. So she's not officially my boss yet."

Hoping that my face looked as neutral as possible, I glanced quickly between them and nodded. "That's right."

"Well, that's my cue to leave then." Quinn wiped her face with a napkin, grabbed her backpack off the floor, and jumped up. "I wanted to go check out that new bookshop anyway. See you at home, Uncle Reid."

Home?

"It was nice to meet you, Avery." The girl flashed me a smile. "He's right, you know. You really are pretty when you smile. I hope whatever made you sad isn't too bad."

My mouth dropped open, but still, I somehow managed to say goodbye and wait until Quinn had made her exit before I let my smile slip away again.

"Okay," Reid said as soon as we were alone. "Are you going to tell me what's going on? Because if you decided to hire Danny Davis after all—"

"I'm not hiring anyone." I stopped him. "I'm going to lose the inn."

Chapter Eleven

Reid

THERE IS no way I heard her correctly.

"You're what?"

Unshed tears shone in her eyes when she looked up again. "I'm…"

"Come on." I grabbed her hand and pulled her up from the table to lead her out of the shop. I threw up a hand to wave goodbye to Craig, who was behind the counter and led Avery out into the spring air of the plaza.

And just in time because the moment we were in the fresh air, tears started to fall from her eyes. She swiped at her face with the back of her hand. "I'm sorry. I didn't want to…thank you." She accepted the napkin I'd swiped from the table and dabbed at her eyes. "I can't believe I'm crying. It's all just…"

"It's okay." I didn't know whether that was true or not, but it seemed like the right thing to say when someone burst into tears in front of you. "Whatever it is, I'm sure it'll be—"

"I don't have a husband."

Of all the things that could have come out of Avery's mouth, I wasn't expecting that. Mostly because it hadn't occurred to me for even a second that she *might* have a husband.

With a breath, I took a step closer to her and lifted her chin gently with my thumb. "I don't know why that's got you so upset," I said as gently as I could manage. "But I'm sure as hell glad you don't have one."

Avery's face flushed, and to my surprise, she burst out laughing. "I'm not really sure what to say about that." She wiped at her eyes and blew out a breath. "But I think you're going to change your opinion when I tell you why it matters."

Her lips turned down in a frown I'd never seen on her pretty face. She glanced around us at the busy plaza with people coming and going. It wasn't the most private setting to have what was quickly shaping up to be a serious conversation.

"Come on." I took her hand and led her down the pedestrian-only street.

A handful of people I knew waved and said hi as we passed. I ignored every single one of them, focused only on Avery and whatever had happened since I'd seen her that morning.

Finally, we arrived at the park benches that looked out over the creek that ran alongside the plaza shopping area that was filled with cafes and shops. It was as private as we were going to get for now.

Avery sat next to me on the bench and turned so she faced me, our knees almost touching. Not wanting to rush her, I gave her a minute to compose herself. However, patience was not one of my virtues, and trying to figure out why she was upset about not having a husband was starting to make me crazy.

With immense patience, I waited until she was ready. Finally, she blew out a breath. "I'm not really sure how to say this."

"I've always found that saying what you need to say with as little bullshit as possible works the best."

I wasn't trying to be funny, but it felt fucking good when her lips finally curled up into a smile, no matter how small.

"Right. Well, in that case. Here it is." She straightened her shoulders, and my eyes dropped to the tantalizing line of cleavage that her wrap dress showed off.

My dick had no business reacting the way he did when she was clearly distraught. But he had a mind of his own. It's not like I could do anything about my semi currently straining against the fly of my jeans. At least not until I was alone.

"I'm going to lose the inn," she said matter-of-factly. "I'm sorry I wasted your time. But I can't hire you after all."

And just like that, the blood returned to my brain, and she had my full attention. "What the fuck?"

"That's what I said." She tried to smile, but it didn't reach her eyes. "Turns out that when my grandparents wrote their will, I was only a little girl and because they come from a different generation, they just assumed that by the time they passed away, I'd be married."

Her distress over not having a husband was quickly coming into focus.

"You're not married."

She looked me in the eye and told me what I already knew. "I'm not."

I couldn't pretend I didn't like that little fact. A lot. Avery and her bubbly, over-the-top personality were pretty much everything I tried to avoid in life. Never mind the fact that she was a city girl who didn't belong in my small town, changing things up. But despite those two very big strikes against her, I was really starting to like the woman.

And my dick...well, we'd already established his thoughts on the matter.

"Okay, you're going to have to expand on this a little," I said after a moment. "How does all this translate to you losing the inn?" And me losing my job. The job I needed to cover the deposit I put down on the shop earlier today.

"I was so sure it wasn't going to," she said. "But I had the lawyer look into it, and there's no way around it. If I don't have a husband, I don't inherit the inn or the savings account put aside to fix it up. And..." She lifted her left hand in the air and wiggled it before dropping it to her lap in defeat. "That's not likely to happen in the next few days. So..." She turned and stared out over the creek, lost in her thoughts.

I watched for a moment while fresh tears rolled down her cheeks, trying to make sense of everything she'd just told me.

No husband. No inn. No job. No money. No shop.

Fuck.

"I guess there's only one thing to do then."

Avery spun around and stared at me. "Reid. I already told you—"

"Marry me."

Avery

"Marry you?"

There was no way he just said that. The stress must be getting to me because there was no way I heard him say that.

"Yes." His face was serious. No trace of a smile. He wasn't joking when he said it again. "Marry me."

What. The. Actual...

My mouth opened and shut like a fish, but no words came out. I pressed my lips together, took a breath, and tried again. Still, there were no words.

There was once a time when I imagined my wedding proposal a million different times in a million different ways, and not once had this particular scenario come up.

Not even close.

"Avery." Reid grabbed my hand; his touch somehow grounded me and brought me back into the moment. "You need a husband, and I..."

What did he need?

His eyes darted back and forth, before landing on mine once more. "I need the money," he said after a moment.

"Money?"

I don't know why, but the admission stung a little. Which was absolutely bonkers because it wasn't as if this man, who I hardly knew and I didn't even really think *liked* me, had actually proposed marriage for any other reason than personal gain.

"You want me to pay you to be my—"

"No!" He squeezed my hand and reached for the other one. "It's not like that. I need this job. That's all. Nothing extra."

It was hard to think with him sitting so close. And the touch of his hands on mine was doing all kinds of things to my insides. Things I had absolutely no business feeling. Especially now.

"Wait." I pulled away and jumped to my feet. I needed space to think. Space away from his manly, warm scent that was obviously clouding my better judgment. "You're not serious." I turned around to face him and the expression on his face that didn't give me any other indication. "Are you?"

Reid crossed one leg over the other and leaned back with his arms extended on the bench behind him as he nodded. "Very."

"You want to marry me?"

"I want you to keep the inn."

"Because you need a job."

"And you need the inn."

So many thoughts raced through my head. I needed a minute to make sense of them. "But a few days ago, you didn't even want the job."

"Things changed."

"What things?"

He tipped his head, looking so cocky and sure of himself that of course I would say yes to his...*proposal.* If that's what it really was.

"I told you." Reid shrugged. "I need the money."

64

"Badly enough that you'll marry me for it?"

He looked me straight in the eyes and nodded.

Damn. He must really need that money.

But I needed him.

Well, I needed his skills.

His *handyman* skills. I couldn't afford to think about what other skills Reid might have. My entire body tingled with the suggestion.

"What does this even look like?" The question surprised even me, because what I really should have said was no. Absolutely not. Who gets fake married to the grumpy handyman who barely even likes them just to keep an inn?

Me, apparently.

Dammit, Carrie was right. I *was* living a Hallmark movie.

Chapter Twelve

Reid

I'M GOING TO HELL.

There was no way around it.

By the time I got Avery to sit down and work out the details of our *marriage*, I had already convinced myself that this was the perfect solution to get exactly what I wanted. Sure, she'd get what she wanted, too. But if I was being perfectly honest with myself, that didn't really factor into why I suggested the union.

I needed that shop.

I needed this job.

Therefore, I needed Avery.

A fact that my dick was in one hundred percent in agreement with.

But he'd have to calm the fuck down because that's not what this marriage was about.

"It'll have to look real." Over the last ten minutes, Avery had slowly come around to my idea and was now focused on some of the finer details. "If it doesn't, I have a cousin who will jump at the chance to blow this up." She shook her head, concern wrinkling on her brow. "I can't go through all of this just to lose it in the end."

"Agreed. It'll look real." How hard could it be? Pretending to be married to Avery didn't seem like it would be a hardship. "I'm sure you have an extra room in that inn that I can move into."

"Oh."

"I will have to move in, Avery."

"Right." She nodded. "Obviously."

"It'll be easier to get the work done that way, too. I can work longer hours and—"

"Will that be part of the deal?" Avery ran her hands through her hair, pulling it up into a ponytail before letting it fall again around her shoulders.

Such an innocent move, but damn if it didn't make me want to pull my bride-to-be into my arms and show her exactly what some of the advantages to being married to me —fake or not—could be.

I forced myself to pay attention to what she was saying.

"I don't want it to get awkward if…well, any *more* awkward by paying you by the hour. Maybe we should do a flat rate. Like half now and half when it's all over."

That made sense to me. I did the rough calculations in my head. The first installment would be more than enough to cover the deposit and the first few payments on the new shop space. Maybe even get me a few new tools. "Deal."

"We'll need an actual marriage certificate," she said. "It has to be legal."

"No problem. I know Judge Baker. He'll do the ceremony. I can get the marriage certificate tomorrow."

She blinked rapidly as that sank in.

We were doing this.

"And your family?"

"Oh." My brothers could potentially be a problem. Mostly because they were always up in my business. And annoyingly, they always seemed to think they knew me better than I knew myself. "I don't usually involve my family with my relationships."

It wasn't a lie. I'd never brought a woman home to meet my family, but only because I'd never dated anyone seriously. Hookups? Yes. Fuck buddies? Also, yes. Girlfriends? No. And definitely not anything that might resemble a relationship.

At least not since senior year and Isabella Hendricks. I loved that girl, and I would have done anything for her. Correction: I *had* done everything for her. Including turning down my college acceptance so I could stay in Trickle Creek with her.

Three months after graduation, Isabella hooked up with a rich city kid on vacation with his family, fucked him in *my* truck that she'd "needed to borrow," and gotten herself knocked up.

Last I heard, she was divorced with three kids and a huge alimony payment. Good for her. But, yeah, I hadn't bothered with anything that came close to a relationship since.

Fool me once, and all that.

"They'll buy it," I told Avery. "Plus, they'll be so fucking happy that someone will have my grumpy ass, they'll be all for it."

"And your niece?"

Shit.

I hated to lie to Quinn. My brothers were different. And with my mom down in Arizona, I was pretty sure I could handle her questions easily enough. At least for a little while. But Quinn was different.

"She liked you." It wasn't a lie, but I didn't bother telling Avery that earlier that afternoon, I'd made a point to tell my niece that Avery and I were not and would not be dating. I'd have to figure out how to work my way out of that.

"Okay then." Her pretty smile was back on her face.

I hadn't realized just how much I'd missed it until that moment. Fuck, she was gorgeous.

"It's settled then."

"I guess so." I reached for her, suddenly unsure of how to seal such a deal. *Did we kiss on it? Shaking hands seemed a little cold. But—*

"Reid Lyons!" The sharp and unmistakable voice of Tilley Beckett rang out right as I grabbed Avery's hand.

"Tilley," I said. "It's nice to see you." That was a lie. Although there was nothing inherently bad about Tilley, the older woman always seemed to appear at the most inopportune time. She knew everything about everyone and loved nothing more than sharing any and all details with everybody she came across.

At the same time, Tilley was probably the most beloved citizen of Trickle Creek. Despite her incessant need to gossip, she truly didn't have a bad bone in her body. She volunteered for everything, including things you didn't even know needed doing.

Still. She was the very last person that I wanted to see at the exact moment Avery and I were about to finalize the details for our fake marriage.

"Who is this pretty young thing?" Tilley ignored my attempt at pleasantries and homed in on Avery immediately.

Without missing a beat, Avery stood and offered the old woman her hand. "Avery Walker. My grandparents were—"

"Sue and Tommy Walker!" Tilley grasped Avery's hand. "Well, I haven't seen you since you were a little girl. Such lovely people, your grandparents. I was so sorry to hear about your grandfather's passing. And the two of you..." She gestured between us. "It's been a few years since you two knew each other."

Avery and I exchanged glances, but before either of us could ask what the older woman was talking about, Tilley continued.

"Your grandmother used to take you boys over to play in the gardens with little Avery while she and Sue would sit on that swing, drinking lemonade and catching up." Tilley's face grew wistful for a moment before her head snapped up. "Surely you remember the way you'd pick all the daisies and give them to little Avery? Or maybe that was Grayson..."

Something in the very back of my memory flashed. Sure, I remember being at the inn, and there had been a little girl sometimes, but...could that have been Avery?

Next to me, she gripped my arm and when I looked down into her eyes, I could see that she was coming to the same realization. We'd known each other as kids.

"It has been a while," Avery said. "But things have a

funny way of working out." She looked right at me as she spoke, and I couldn't help but believe that maybe this whole crazy situation would work out.

"Avery is going to be restoring the inn," I blurted out. With any luck, Tilley would take the tidbit of info and rush off immediately to spread the news.

"Is that right?" She looked between the two of us. "I did hear a rumor that someone had returned to town to do just that. I didn't realize it was you. It must be my lucky day, running into the two of you today."

Tilley flashed me a grin, and I saw something spark in her eyes. "I wasn't interrupting anything important between the two of you, was I?" She wiggled her wiry, white eyebrows.

There was no help for it, and considering we'd already committed to it, it seemed that there was no time like the present. I slipped my arm around Avery's waist and pulled her close to me. "Well, since you asked…" I looked at my bride-to-be. She shrugged and offered me a half smile, so I went for it. "I guess you're going to be the first to know, Tilley." The whole town would know within the hour. "Seeing Avery again after all those years brought back feelings we didn't even know we had." Okay, it was a little white lie. "And just a moment ago, Avery agreed to make me a very happy man, and be my wife."

I squeezed her a little tighter and dropped a chaste kiss on the top of her head.

Tilley's face lit up, and she clapped her hands together in glee.

It was done.

For better or worse.

Chapter Thirteen

Reid

THE LAST THING I wanted to do the night before my wedding—real or not—was spend it with my brothers.

The irony wasn't lost on me, because, in almost any other scenario, that's exactly how I'd want to spend the night before getting married. My brothers were my best friends. We were a close family.

Annoyingly so at times.

Which was exactly why dinner at Brody's house was going to be unbearable. I had no doubt that news of my *engagement* had made its rounds through town. The fact that my phone hadn't already been blowing up with text messages and calls demanding an explanation from Grayson, Brody, Preston, and Ethan could only mean one thing.

They were planning an ambush. Or an intervention.

Either way, I wasn't looking forward to it.

I knocked twice on the front door of the house we grew

up in. After Dad died and Mom remarried and moved south, my oldest brother Brody bought the house, which made it a handy and somewhat familiar gathering spot when we got together.

At times—like now—it felt like I was sixteen again, getting called out for skipping class or coming home late.

All four of my brothers were already in the kitchen when I walked in.

"Am I late?"

I wasn't.

Preston, the youngest, handed me a bottle of beer. "Good to see you."

I took it with a nod of thanks and tipped it to my lips. Judging by the atmosphere in the room, I was going to need it.

No one said anything for a few minutes. I was almost half done with my beer before Brody spoke up. "You're always welcome to bring your fiancée to family dinner."

Even though I was expecting it, I almost choked on my beer.

"After all," Brody continued. "She's family now."

"*Almost* family." It was my twin who made the clarification.

Unlike the others, Grayson wasn't smiling.

Fuck.

There were a lot of details I hadn't considered when I proposed our little arrangement to Avery. My brothers and how they might react were definitely one of the bigger ones.

"Feel like filling us in on some of the details, brother?" Ethan leaned back in his chair. "Like, maybe…who she is?"

"She's a super cute blonde." Grayson spoke up, his face

still an unreadable mask. "She just inherited the Tamarack Inn from her grandparents and moved back to town." He lifted his bottle to his lips and took a drink before continuing. "What? A week ago or so?"

"Almost three weeks ago, now."

"Feels pretty quick, don't you think?"

I stared directly into the eyes that were identical to my own. "When you know, you know. And it's really not that quick after all. We've known each other since we were kids."

Grayson shot me a look.

"Remember when Grandma would take us over to the inn in the summers while she visited with Mrs. Walker?" There was a flicker of remembrance on my brother's face. "We'd run around the gardens and there was always a little girl there, too."

"No shit?"

I nodded. "So really, we've known each other most of our lives." Grayson opened his mouth to object, but I didn't give him a chance. "Besides, if I'm not mistaken, you were more or less pushing Avery on me. I guess I have you to thank for all this."

He didn't look away. "I guess congratulations are in order."

"Thank you."

Guilt flared through me, but I worked to keep it off my face. I'd never lied to Grayson before. There wouldn't have been any point to it anyway. We'd always been so close, he could see right through any and all of my bullshit.

If he could see it now, he wasn't saying.

"So?" Preston pulled my attention away from my twin.

"What's she like? She must be pretty special if she managed to melt your frozen heart."

"My heart is not frozen."

"No," Preston agreed. "Just hard."

"Like a rock." Brody laughed. "Seriously, she must be some kind of magical to break through your walls so quickly."

Magical? Maybe not. But special? Abso-fucking-lutely.

"Quinn said she was pretty," Ethan offered. "And really nice. She said that you all had ice cream yesterday."

"Was that before or after your engagement?"

I ignored Grayson and focused on Ethan.

"We did." I glanced around the kitchen. "Where is Quinn? We need to talk about how she hears *everything*. That kid is always listening." And I needed to pull my niece aside and try to explain this new situation to her.

"She's at a friend's." Ethan shrugged. "And yes, she is a good little spy."

"Right." I drained the last of my beer, set the bottle on the counter, and lifted an eyebrow. "That works both ways, brother. She mentioned something about my potential and how I needed a good woman."

Ethan burst out laughing. "I can't speak for your potential, but it sounds like maybe you've got a good woman now."

"She's a good one, all right," Grayson said. "No idea what a cute little blonde with a smile that bright saw in a grump like you, but...cheers, Reid. If you're happy, I'm happy."

"Is Reid ever really happy?" Preston ducked out of the

way of my fist. "Seriously, bro. We're happy. Even if it is a ridiculously quick engagement. I can't wait to meet her."

"I bet Mom's pretty excited."

That was the other big factor I hadn't given enough consideration. *Mom.* I blew out a breath and grabbed a bun from the basket Brody was setting out. "Yeah, I haven't told Mom yet." I tore off a piece. "I thought I'd wait until she came up to visit this fall."

"This fall? Is that when the wedding will be?"

Fuck.

I stuffed the piece in my mouth and dropped the rest of the bun on the plate.

"Reid?"

"About that," I finally said. "I actually can't stay tonight because…well, tomorrow's the big day and I—"

"What the fuck?"

"Tomorrow?"

"Is she knocked up?"

The room erupted into chaos with everyone speaking at once.

I waited until my brothers quieted down a bit before offering up a little more information. "No, Avery isn't pregnant." We would have had to have sex for that to happen. And as much as my evenings were filled with fantasies of that very thing, that's all they'd been—fantasies. "We just don't want to wait." I slowly backed away from the table. "It's not a big deal or anything. We're just going to have a small thing at the courthouse for now. Maybe we'll have a big reception in a few months."

We had no intention of having a big party because if everything went according to plan, the marriage would be dissolved by then. But if this was going to work, we had to keep up appearances. They had to believe it. Everyone did.

After returning to the inn yesterday, Avery and I had gone over the plan, such as it was. And we'd decided it was easier not to tell anyone the truth. Especially in a town this size. It had to remain a secret if it was going to work. At least until all the papers were signed and the inn was legally hers.

"We're not very traditional."

All four of my brothers stared at me in silence and for the first time, I thought maybe I was going to be called on my immense amount of bullshit.

Finally, it was Brody who spoke first. "That actually seems pretty on-brand for you, Reid. I'll be honest. I didn't expect to ever see this day at all. But this adds up."

Preston nodded in agreement, and Ethan shrugged. "He's not wrong. And hell, the only thing that matters is that the two of you are happy."

"I appreciate that." I accepted his offer of a quick hug. "Really, Ethan. Thanks, man."

Brody and Preston followed suit, offering me their well wishes, and then it was just Grayson.

"I'll walk you out." He moved past me before I could object.

With a wave to the rest of my brothers, I followed Grayson out to the porch, bracing myself.

The screen door slapped shut behind me. "Hey, about all of this...I'm really—"

"You'll need a witness tomorrow." His jaw twitched.

I could see there was so much he wanted to say. The fact

that he didn't was a testament to our relationship and the trust between us.

Trust that I was fucking with.

I hoped like hell he'd understand.

"Two o'clock. At the courthouse."

Grayson nodded. "I'll be there."

Chapter Fourteen

Avery

AS FAR AS I could tell, there wasn't a dress code for a fake wedding to a man you hardly knew, and considering I hadn't packed very much with me when I came to Trickle Creek, my options were pretty limited.

I settled on a pale-green dress with a sweetheart neckline that flared from the hip with a hem that danced around my knees.

Reid told me he'd handle the arrangements, and we'd agreed to meet at the little courthouse at ten to two.

I'd almost talked myself out of going through with this insane plan at least twenty times the night before. But ultimately, when I looked around the inn, I knew there was only one way to keep it. I was almost one hundred percent sure that my grandparents would want me to have the inn, even if it meant that it took a little deception to get it.

In this instance, the ends truly did justify the means.

Besides, it wasn't like anyone was going to get hurt.

Reid and I were both consenting adults. He'd get the money he wanted and I'd get the inn. It was a win-win.

If all went well, we could get the divorce or annulment or whatever it took in a few months and go about our lives as if nothing had happened.

I straightened my dress and brushed off some imaginary lint with one last look in the old mirror. I'd never been one of those little girls who spent hours imagining their wedding day or dressing up in my mother's old wedding gown. To be fair, the only time I'd ever given a wedding any thought at all was when Porter and I got serious.

Then I thought about it. Maybe more than I cared to remember.

I'd pictured walking down the aisle to my smiling groom, who thought I was the best, most beautiful woman in the entire world and couldn't be happier and prouder to become my husband. I imagined a room full of friends and family, all crying happy tears for us. A white dress, flowers, and little lights everywhere while we danced our first dance together.

When that didn't happen, well...I stopped thinking about marriage altogether. But if I had, the one nonnegotiable would be love.

I sighed at my reflection before shaking my head and scolding myself. There was no need to be dramatic about it. Just because I was marrying Reid today didn't mean I wouldn't marry for love later on.

That sounded so fucked up, even in my head.

Before I could let myself go any further down that train of thought, I checked the time.

Fucked up or not, it was time to go.

. . .

Like most things in Trickle Creek, the walk to the courthouse only took a few minutes. Minutes that only increased my anxiety and had me second-guessing everything.

But there was no turning back.

Reid was already there. He hadn't seen me yet and had his back to me. If I wanted to change my mind, now was the time.

I took a breath and exhaled slowly.

No. I wasn't going to change my mind.

"Ready for this?"

He turned around.

Reflexively, I took a step backward.

"I should be asking you that."

Confused, the smile I'd pasted on my face slipped off, but only for a second before I realized it wasn't my future husband in front of me. "Grayson."

His face split in a smile. "Hey there, Avery. Or should I call you sister?"

We'd talked about keeping the truth of our marriage under wraps, but I hadn't even thought about what it would mean for his family to believe the wedding was real. It felt wrong on more than one level.

"There's no way I was going to miss this." Grayson's warm smile, so opposite his brother's permanent grimace, put me at ease immediately. "I'm not going to pretend to understand it, Avery." His smile dipped a little, giving me a fresh shot of nerves. "But I think you're great, and if this is what Reid really wants, you both have my support, one hundred percent."

Relief washed through me. Not that I actually thought Grayson was going to confront me in any way, but then again, I didn't know what to expect. I'd never been involved in a situation like this. Before I could respond, the atmosphere shifted around me and a shiver raced down my spine. Turning just confirmed what I already knew.

Reid.

My breath caught in my throat. Until now, I'd only seen him in old jeans and a T-shirt. Not that I was complaining. Reid made them look *good*. But now, dressed in deep-charcoal pants and a jacket with a black button-down, he looked positively edible.

Neither of us spoke. My body heated under his gaze as he took his time looking me up and down. My knees buckled a little, and just when I thought I might make a fool of myself by tripping over my heels, he spoke.

"You look gorgeous, Avery." He cleared his throat as if the compliment had taken too much effort and thrust a small bouquet at me. "Here."

"Oh." I took the cluster of peonies from him and lifted it to my nose. "They're beautiful, thank you."

Reid shrugged as if it wasn't a big deal, but it was. And not just because peonies were one of my favorites.

"I thought you should have a bouquet for…well."

"Your wedding day?"

We both jolted, remembering that Grayson was still standing there and as far as he knew, we were so madly in love we couldn't wait to tie the knot.

I recovered first. "Of course I do." I flashed him a smile

and tossed my hair over my shoulder. "They're perfect, Reid." I stood on my tiptoes and pressed a kiss to his cheek.

It was the most innocent touch, but fire sparked from my lips and lit something low in my gut. Something that made my knees weak when Reid snaked his arm around my waist and pulled me close.

He looked down into my eyes as if we were the only two people in the world. "Are you ready to do this, Avery?"

I blinked.

"Ready to be my wife?"

The word hung heavy between us. I didn't take my eyes off him while I gave my heart a moment to stop racing.

His hand splayed across my lower back and he didn't rush me.

Finally, my lips curled up, and I nodded. With a courage that mingled with an unexpected flash of desire for my husband-to-be, I smiled. "Let's do this."

Reid

I couldn't take my eyes off her. Avery was always stunning, but somehow, standing in front of me in that green dress that made her eyes pop, with just a trace of cleavage that should have been chaste yet somehow made my dick hard in a completely inappropriate for the situation way, made her absolutely breathtaking.

She clutched her flowers tight and nodded every once in a while to something that Judge Baker said, paying close attention to everything that came out of the man's mouth.

That made one of us.

He was talking too much, and I wasn't paying attention to anything that came out of his mouth. All I could focus on was Avery and the fact that in a few minutes, she was going to be my wife.

Wife.

Holy shit. That's not a word I ever thought I'd use.

"Reid, take Avery's hands," the judge said, pulling me back to the moment.

She turned and handed Grayson her bouquet. I watched as my twin gave her a kind smile before his eyes met mine.

He hadn't said a word about it, but I could feel his skepticism like a weight on my shoulders. He had questions. A lot of them. But he was proving himself to be an excellent fucking brother with the fact that he hadn't asked me a single one.

I gave him a nod and reached for Avery's hands.

They were soft and delicate, dwarfed by my rough ones. But the grip she gave was firm, like she needed to ground herself. I squeezed her back in solidarity, and she smiled.

Fuck, I loved that smile.

Her eyes met mine as Judge Baker once more began talking. His words blurred together, something about promises and forever, but I barely heard him over the thumping of my heart and the hum of something more that was building between us.

"Reid?"

"What?" Reluctantly, I tore my gaze away from Avery long enough to look at the judge, who stared at me.

The older man chuckled before repeating himself. "Do the two of you have vows you'd like to share with each other at this time?"

Shit.

Avery looked just as shocked as I did. We hadn't even considered vows.

"No," I answered for both of us. "We don't."

To his credit, Judge Baker didn't look surprised. "And rings?" He glanced between us. "Are there rings?"

Shit.

This time, Avery didn't look caught off guard. She released my hand long enough to reach into a pocket in her dress and produce two simple gold bands.

I looked at her in question, but she only shrugged.

The judge smiled and nodded. "Reid. Place the ring on Avery's left ring finger."

I did as instructed.

"Now, do you take this woman to be your lawfully wedded wife? Do you promise to keep her in sickness and health, for richer or for poorer, for better or for worse, as long as you both shall live?"

"Yes," I said without hesitation. "I mean…" Once more, I looked into Avery's eyes. "I do."

A blush crept over her cheeks.

"And you, Avery," Judge Baker said, "place the ring on Reid's finger."

She did, the smooth metal warm from her touch.

"Do you take this man to be your lawfully wedded husband? Do you promise to keep him in sickness and health, for richer or for poorer, for better or for worse, as long as you both shall live?"

She swallowed hard, but her eyes never left mine as she said, "I do."

We did.

The judge was once again talking. This time, all I heard was, "I now pronounce you husband and wife. Reid, you may kiss your bride."

Avery's breath hitched. Mine did, too. This was the part that mattered. The part that sealed it.

I took a step to close the gap between us and cupped my hand gently over her cheek. I dipped my head to hers, catching the faint inhale from her before my lips met hers.

Soft. Warm. So fucking perfect.

Her lips yielded to mine and what was meant to be just a brush of lips turned very quickly into something else entirely.

Her hands curled into mine. I tilted my head, deepening the kiss without thinking. A move that was reciprocated, when the slightest moan slipped from her lips.

I forgot Grayson. I forgot the judge and his assistant who was acting as a witness. I forgot that this wasn't real.

I forgot everything except the woman in my arms.

My wife.

It was my brother who cleared his throat, causing Avery to take a step back. Her chest fell in quick, shallow breaths. Her lips slightly parted, and her bright-blue eyes blazed with something I couldn't quite name, but it sure as hell wasn't indifference.

"That was…something," Grayson said with a low whistle. "Maybe you're not as crazy as I thought."

I turned to glare at him, but the heat in my face wasn't annoyance—it was from the way Avery was still looking at me. Like I just turned her entire world upside down.

Fuck.

She wasn't the only one.

Chapter Fifteen

Avery

THE TRUCK RUMBLED to a stop in the driveway, and for a moment, neither of us moved. With my peonies still clutched in my hands, I stared out the window at the inn and its weathered, peeling paint and sagging porch. My gaze landed on my broken swing, still in a heap where I'd left it.

There was so much work still to do.

Not that there was any *more* work than there had been that morning, but now, somehow it felt different. The weight of everything that still needed to be done, combined with what had just happened, weighed heavy.

This was home now—for both of us.

I turned to Reid, but he was already climbing out of the truck, his jaw tight as he grabbed the duffel bag he'd brought with him. He hadn't said much since the kiss.

The. Kiss.

Of course, there was going to be a kiss. It was a

wedding, after all. It was kind of required. But…damn. I had not expected that.

My stomach twisted at the memory of his hand cupping my cheek with a tenderness I didn't know he was capable of.

Fake, I reminded myself. Not for the first time since it happened.

Still, the memory of his lips, warm and firm on mine, lingered in the back of my mind.

I followed him to the porch and dug through my tiny purse to find the new keys I'd made.

"You lock it?"

"Of course, I lock it."

He chuckled and shook his head a little. "It's Trickle Creek, Avery. I don't know what you think will happen. But nothing will. Nobody locks their doors around here."

"Just a habit, I guess." I slipped the key in the door easily, unlike the first time Reid and I met, and turned the door handle. "Welcome home…I guess."

He didn't reply. Reid only stood there, looming over me with an unreadable brooding expression on his face that made it completely impossible to tell what he was thinking.

"Am I supposed to carry you over the threshold or something?"

I couldn't help it; a laugh slipped out. "Are you serious?"

He grunted in response. Despite the shrug, I could see that he was, in fact, serious.

"I don't think it's necessary, to be honest."

"What if someone is watching?"

"Who would be watching?"

Again, he shrugged. "Tilley Beckett."

My eyes widened. "You really think that?"

"I think it's a small town and there are eyes everywhere."

That was fair. I still wasn't used to the way everyone knew everyone and their business in Trickle Creek. "Okay, well—oh!"

Reid scooped me up so quickly and unexpectedly that I almost dropped my flowers. Reflexively, I wrapped my arms around his neck and looked up into his dark eyes.

His lips twitched up into what might have been the start of a smile. "I didn't mean to startle you, wife."

Wife.

I tried not to focus on the word. Or his strong arms that were currently wrapped underneath me, pulling me close into the hard wall of muscle of his chest.

Or his smell.

Something that was pure manliness.

"Here we go." He hitched me a little higher in his arms before easily crossing the threshold into the inn.

Reid kicked the door shut behind him, his eyes never leaving mine.

A shiver ran through me as I looked up at my *husband.*

He might be a giant grump. And this might all be fake. But damn, he was sexy.

I couldn't help but be disappointed when he set me on my feet and took a step back.

The inn smelled of paint and sawdust, two scents I was quickly coming to love because they meant progress was being made.

"I cleared out a room for you. It's the first one on the left." I pointed toward the stairs unnecessarily. "I'm sorry about the bed. I have to order all new mattresses when… well, when the money comes through." I blew out a breath.

"So, you get an air mattress. I hope it's not too uncomfortable."

"It'll be fine." He nodded. "Thank you."

I dropped my hands to my sides. "Well, I'll let you get settled. I'm just…" I looked behind me. Any other night, and I'd probably change into my work clothes and work on something, but it didn't feel quite right to pick up a paintbrush on my wedding night.

Wedding night.

I forced any and all feelings that those words conjured out of my brain.

Reid seemed to sense my discomfort. He hitched the strap of his duffel up on his shoulder and, with a nod, headed toward the stairs. I watched him climb the stairs, a strange sensation of disappointment filling me.

But that was stupid. What did I expect to happen? It was a fake marriage. We hardly knew each other.

Still…

"Reid," I called, the word slipping out before I could stop it.

He stopped, turning halfway to look at me.

"Thanks," I said lamely. "For…well, for all of this," I finished, my voice softer than I intended.

For a moment, his expression softened, just a little, and I thought he might say something. But then he gave a curt nod and kept walking, leaving me standing there watching after him long after he disappeared.

No. This was not exactly how I'd imagined my wedding night would go.

Chapter Sixteen

Reid

WORK on the inn was going faster than I'd expected. Almost too fast when you considered that Avery still hadn't finalized the ownership paperwork.

It wasn't her fault, and I know it was weighing on her, but according to William Evans, these things took time and we had only been married a week. Apparently, that wasn't enough time to process everything.

Avery wasn't saying much about it, but I knew it was worrying her that the paperwork hadn't been completed yet. Not only was the inn not officially hers yet, but that meant that the trust fund that had been created for the project also had not been released yet.

Still, it had only been a week.

A week.

Avery had been my wife for a full week.

Time flies when…well, you're working.

That's pretty much all we'd been doing. Worked on the

inn almost all day, every day with very few breaks. That's probably why we were making such quick progress on things.

Maybe I should slow things down?

After all, the sooner I finished work, the sooner I wouldn't have a reason to hang out with Avery all day, every day, and there was no point denying how much I was enjoying that particular perk of the job.

Sure, she was a city girl—that much was true.

But it bothered me less and less. Every morning, as I worked out the cricks and aches in my back from sleeping on that insufferable air mattress, I looked forward to seeing her bright smile in the kitchen when she handed me a cup of coffee.

Together, we'd sit on the porch steps—the swing still out of commission—and discuss the projects for the day.

We'd break again for lunch and then dinner. And the whole time we worked, we talked. I was used to working in silence, but Avery had a way of easily drawing the conversation out of me. Over painting, sanding, and the hum of the air compressor, we were learning about each other. And the more I learned about Avery, the more I liked.

The little routine we'd established was…nice.

But the best part was in the evenings when we sat on the steps, watching the sunset behind the mountains. I looked forward to those quiet moments the most.

But today, I had something almost as exciting to take care of.

Avery might still be waiting for her paperwork to go through, but mine had. The workshop was officially mine. Well, as long as I kept making payments, it was mine.

But for all intents and purposes, I finally had my own shop where I could build the high-end, custom furniture I'd always wanted to create.

I backed up the truck and trailer, packed with some of the tools I'd loaded up earlier that afternoon with Ethan's help. My brother was as eager to get my stuff out of his shed as I was to get out of there and more than willing to help me pack up before I drove off.

My new shop space was at least five times bigger than the little shed, with giant double doors that I flung open. I stood with my hands on my hips and took it all in with a grin on my face.

"Damn, brother. Did your new wife put that smile on your face, or are you really just that happy to have a workshop of your own?"

I spun to see my oldest brother. Not even Brody's sarcasm could dull this moment. "A little bit of both," I said truthfully. "Thanks for coming to help. This is definitely a two-man job, and Ethan was excited to spread out into the shed."

Brody took a look at the trailer and the heavy equipment. "Looks to me like more than two men wouldn't have been a total waste. Let's get to work."

We worked for the next hour and by the time we had everything moved in, we were both exhausted. I handed Brody a beer from the cooler I'd packed.

"Cheers to you, brother." Brody tapped his can against mine, and we both drank deeply. "This is a big deal." He looked around the still, mostly empty space. Out of all my brothers, I knew Brody would understand what this meant to me.

He'd opened Peak to Path, an outdoors store, in the plaza a few years back. Our youngest brother, Preston, helped him get everything up and running and had even invested a small amount of savings with him. But more often than not, Preston could be found out in the mountains instead of actually working in the shop.

"I know you understand," I said to Brody. "I didn't think it was ever going to happen, but when this space came available, I couldn't pass it up."

"Lucky you had the funds available." He shot me a look.

I tipped the can to my lips and drank deeply before responding. "Is there something you want to ask me?"

Brody hesitated, and I braced myself. Ready for a fight. If my brothers had opinions about my marriage—and I know they did—they'd kept them to themselves so far, and I preferred to keep it that way.

Thankfully, Brody shook his head and lifted his can. "Nope. I was just going to say that it's a damn good thing Avery Walker moved to town when she did with a big project."

I narrowed my eyes, but I wouldn't rise to the bait. "Sure is," I said. "In more ways than one."

It wasn't a lie. Having Avery come to town allowed me to buy this shop. But it was more than that—a lot more.

I wasn't used to working so closely with someone else, at least not someone who wasn't my brother who I could tell to fuck off whenever they irritated me. But with Avery…it was different. Not only did her consistently bright smile and optimism about every single situation *not* irritate me—a miracle in itself—but I liked it.

"So, how's married life?" Brody's question caught me off guard. "You know, we still haven't met your wife. At least not properly."

Shit.

"We've been busy."

"With the inn. Right."

It wasn't a lie. But it also wasn't a good excuse.

"Well, I guess we'll meet her Saturday."

"Saturday?" I almost choked on my beer. "What's happening on Saturday?"

Brody chuckled and crushed his now empty can in his hand before standing. "Only the biggest wedding Trickle Creek has seen in years." He raised one eyebrow with a smug grin on his face. "Craig and Lucy, remember?"

Fuck. With everything going on, I'd completely forgotten. We'd all known Craig and the entire Carlson family our whole lives. Craig was a great guy; he deserved his happiness, and Brody was right. It was going to be a huge wedding. There was no way I could miss it.

"Right." I finished off my own beer and tossed the can into an empty bin. "I guess you'll meet Avery then." I hoped like hell I sounded more confident than I felt about the situation. It was going to be our first event as a married couple and the entire town would be there. It had been easy to keep up the lie when no one was watching, but…could we make it believable with all eyes on us?

It didn't look like we had much of a choice.

Chapter Seventeen

Avery

THE THING no one tells you about restoring an old building was the amount of painting involved. So. Much. Paint.

At this point, it felt like the paintbrush was an extension of my arm.

Not that I minded it too much. Not really.

It was one of the few tasks I could do without Reid's help that made me feel useful. Especially when so much was still out of my control.

Like actually being the owner of the inn officially.

I tried not to think about that one, very crucial detail too much. Especially because there was nothing I could do about it except wait for my lawyer to process the paperwork and hope like hell that my cousin, Jacob, wouldn't screw it all up for me.

Before we could even arrange the funeral, the calls and text messages had begun. And once the will was read, he'd doubled his efforts to make it known that I wasn't the only one interested in owning the inn. The fact that our grandparents had left it to me didn't seem to matter to him.

He'd always resented the closer relationship I had with my grandparents growing up. But that wasn't my fault. If anything, it was his.

As the daughter of a single mom, I'd started spending my summers with them in Trickle Creek when I was pretty young. My aunt and uncle sent him to stay, too. Some of the time. But when we each got old enough to choose, Jacob wasn't interested in visiting a small town and chose instead to go to summer camp or stay in the city with his friends. Of course, my relationship with them grew stronger.

The only time Jacob ever cared about it was on the very few occasions we were all together at a family function. It was only then that his jealousy shone through. And that's all it was. Jealousy.

His parents doted on him to such an extreme that he couldn't stand not being the favorite or the center of attention at all times.

No, this wasn't about him *wanting* the inn. It was about the fact that I had it instead of him.

Not that it mattered. Either way, it was a giant pain in my ass because nothing could proceed as long as he was contesting the will. Which, as of yesterday, was officially what was happening.

William assured me that Jacob didn't have a chance at succeeding considering I was now legally married. Still, I couldn't help but worry that he was going to do everything he could to make things difficult for me.

I dipped the brush in the can a little too aggressively, sloshing paint over the side. "Dammit."

"Looks like you could use a break."

I jumped at Reid's voice and almost kicked over the can of paint entirely.

"Sorry," he said with a chuckle. "I didn't mean to scare you." He crossed the floor and took the brush from my hand. "Why don't you call it quits for the night?"

Given all the mistakes I was making, it didn't seem like a bad idea. "I think that's probably a good choice."

I let Reid put the lid back on the can of paint while I cleaned up my spill. "I thought you were out for the night," I said when we were done. The moment the words were out of my mouth, I wanted them back. It wasn't my job to keep tabs on him. He was free to come and go as he pleased. "I mean, I don't care. It's...fine. You can..."

His eyes flashed and his lips curled up into a small grin, clearly amused at my discomfort. "I went to unload some equipment in my new shop," he offered. "It didn't take as long as I thought. Besides, there's something I want to talk to you about."

My stomach dropped.

"Talk?"

Nothing good ever started with those words. If Reid wanted to pull out of our agreement now, I wouldn't have any chance at keeping the inn. He was my only hope now.

"Oh, I...sure." I tried to smooth my hair back in an effort to look even a little bit put together and in control of the situation.

He shifted his weight, his gaze dropping briefly to the

floor before once more meeting mine. The hesitation on his face made my pulse race, and I had to force myself to take a deep breath.

"Avery." He reached for me. His touch both calmed me and sent my heart on a wild new rhythm. "It's nothing bad." His tone was softer this time. "I promise."

But there was no way I believed him. Not when every nerve in my body was screaming that this was all about to blow up. I swallowed hard and forced my well-practiced smile onto my face. "Okay. Why don't we go sit outside?"

He nodded. "I'll meet you out there."

It was a warm night; spring was quickly turning into summer. Alone on the porch, I took the opportunity to take a few deep breaths and calm myself down. Even if Reid did want out of our agreement, it would be fine. Everything would work out. I knew it would.

It *had* to.

Reid

With two glasses in hand, I stepped out on the porch, expecting to find Avery waiting but she was nowhere to be found. I glanced at the heap of destroyed wood in the corner that used to be her beloved swing. It wasn't high on the priority list, but it would have been a nice place to sit and have this conversation.

At the very least, I could haul away the mess.

But it was a problem for later. I had more important things to discuss with my wife. If I could find her.

I moved to the porch rail and scanned the yard, finally spotting her on the grass, standing next to the old wooden sign.

She had her back to me as I approached. Her fingers grazed over the old, weathered wood. The paint had most peeled off, but the carved words were still easy to read.

Not wanting to startle her, I cleared my throat. "Figured you could use this." I held out a glass when she turned.

"Thanks." She accepted the glass with a small smile and turned back to the sign. "I guess we should put this on the list, too."

I nodded and took a sip. "Are you keeping the name?"

Avery exhaled slowly before turning to face me. "I think so. But there's part of me that wants to make it my own."

I nodded. That made sense.

"But…" She tilted her head toward the backyard. "See those trees?"

I followed her gaze past the house where two tall larch trees stood side by side, their branches swaying a little in the evening breeze. They were full, their soft needles green for the summer. But in the fall, they'd turn a brilliant bright yellow before dropping their needles for the winter. The only coniferous trees to do so, larches were spectacularly beautiful. They'd be a perfect backdrop for the freshly painted inn in a few months.

"They're beautiful trees," I said honestly.

"My grandparents planted them when they opened the inn." Her voice was soft. "They told me the trees were a symbol of strength and togetherness but also change because every year the larches would drop their needles and prepare for a new season."

"It sounds like your grandparents put a lot of heart into this place."

"They did." She took a sip of wine, watching the trees with an expression I couldn't quite read. "They built something they thought would last. I think that's why I'm struggling with all this. The renovations, the name…" She waved a hand and let it drop to her side. "I just want to get it right, you know?"

"You will." I studied her for a moment. She was determined—that much I already knew—but there was something else behind her words. Passion. Love.

Any lingering concerns I might have had that Avery was going to come into town and change this place, the way so many other city folk did, vanished in that moment. She cared. Deeply.

"Do you really think so?" She turned to me, her eyes searching mine.

"I do." I meant it. "It's easy to see how you feel about this place. And no matter what you decide, it's still yours, and your grandparents will be proud. It doesn't have to look exactly the way they left it. But it has to mean something to you."

"Wow." Avery breathed out a small laugh. "That almost sounded wise."

"Don't get used to it." I shook my head and took a sip of my wine.

She smiled again and turned back to the trees.

I let the silence stretch between us, the weight of the history of the place settling between us. For a moment, I could picture the trees, now tall and strong, the way her grandparents would have seen them when they planted them. Small, full of promise and hope.

After a moment, Avery broke the silence. "Sorry. Didn't you say you had something you needed to talk to me about?"

Avery

I'd been so distracted by my own thoughts, that I'd almost forgotten that Reid wanted to talk to me about something.

Almost.

Together, we made our way back to the porch.

"Okay," I said when we finally sat down on the steps. "Lay it on me. What do you need to talk to me about?"

"I told you it's not bad."

I tilted my head in skepticism, and he laughed.

"Really. It's not." His eyes crinkled in the corners when he laughed.

It was incredibly sexy.

"I thought it would be nice to have a glass of wine with my wife."

"Your wife?"

"You *are* my wife, are you not?" He looked over the rim of his glass at me.

"I am," I said. "Unless you brought me out here to ask for a divorce."

"A divorce?" Reid almost spilled his wine. "Why would I want that? Is everything settled with the inn already?"

Immediately, I felt stupid for jumping to conclusions. Reid wasn't the type of man who would go back on his word. The more I got to know him, the more I could see that he was a solid guy. Dependable. And…well, good. Truly, I didn't think he'd do anything to hurt me or go back on the deal we'd made.

"I don't know." I shook my head. "I think just the way you…well, right before you got here, I was thinking about my cousin and how he's trying so hard to screw me over and…" To my horror, tears sprang to my eyes.

"Hey." Reid set his glass of wine down, shifted closer to me on the step, and put his arm around me.

I stiffened for a moment, but his touch was so welcome, so needed, I sank into it and let myself accept the comfort.

"It'll be okay, Avery."

"You don't know him." Hell, I hardly knew my cousin anymore, if I ever really had. But what I did know of him was that he was an asshole.

"We're married," Reid said. "We did it in front of a judge and witnesses. No one can deny that."

I closed my eyes and inhaled his masculine woodsy scent, letting it calm me before I sat up and took a sip of wine. "That's true."

"It sure is." The corner of his mouth quirked up, just enough to make my chest tighten. He didn't smile often, but when it did, it hit like a punch. "You're my wife."

"Wife?"

"You are." He shot me a look. "That's what being married means."

I couldn't help but laugh. "I know that. But you don't usually…well, it's just…"

"Speaking of weddings."

"Were we?"

He lifted an eyebrow and blew out a breath. "We need to make an appearance," he said. "An old friend is getting married. It's going to be a pretty big deal and—"

"You want me to go to a wedding with you?"

"Well, if you don't, the whole town will be talking about it."

I knew that was true. Not only had news of our nuptials spread almost before I could blink, but I couldn't go anywhere in town without people introducing themselves and asking questions that I'm sure they thought were innocent enough. But I could see right through them for the nosiness they really were. People were curious about us. I couldn't blame them.

"Okay," I agreed with a nod. "When is the big day?" I lifted my glass to my lips. It was one thing to pretend to be married in the privacy of the inn, but going out in public...

"This Saturday."

I almost spat out my wine.

"As in, two days from now?"

He nodded, and I laughed.

"Do you think we can pull it off?" I said after a moment.

"Yes." Reid didn't hesitate. "But I do think we should practice first."

"Practice?" I echoed, my pulse kicking up a notch.

He shifted a little on the step, his knees bumping into mine.

"What kind of practice are we talking about?" My voice was softer now.

He leaned back slightly, tipping his head toward mine. "For starters...we should work on the whole *happy couple* thing. So, maybe a kiss."

My breath caught. "A kiss?" I'd be lying if I said I hadn't thought about kissing Reid again. How could I not? He was sexy and strong and…we'd been working so closely together. And then there was the memory of our kiss at the courthouse that played on an almost constant loop in my head, especially when I was alone in my bed at the end of the day.

"We want it to look real." His lips twitched, almost like he was trying not to smile.

"We do," I agreed, leaning closer to him. "And practice *does* make perfect, after all."

He nodded as his rough palm slid over my cheek, cupping it gently. "Really," he said. "It's the responsible thing to do."

He was so close I could feel the warmth of his breath against my lips.

"It is." My voice was little more than a sigh as our lips met.

The kiss started soft—so soft it almost undid me. My heart stuttered, an ache building in my chest.

But then it shifted. Reid angled his head, deepening the kiss with a confidence that sent a shiver down my spine. His hand slipped to the nape of my neck, his thumb brushing against the tender skin there in a way that made me melt into him.

I couldn't stop the small sound that escaped me, just as I couldn't stop leaning into him. My fingers curled into his shirt, holding on to him for balance—or just to ground myself somehow before I got completely lost in him.

Everything around us faded. Nothing else mattered but this man and this moment.

When he finally pulled back, I was breathless. He rested

his forehead against mine and for a long moment, neither of us moved.

"That," he said, his voice rougher now, "felt real enough to me."

I blinked up at him. "Me too."

The way his eyes searched mine told me that this wasn't just practice—not for either of us.

Chapter Eighteen

Reid

I'D NEVER GIVEN weddings much thought. Or any thought at all, to be honest. I'm a guy. Guys don't give a shit about weddings unless they were their own. Even then, it was debatable.

But even I had to admit, Craig and Lucy's wedding was beautiful. It felt like the entire town was in attendance for the nuptials that were held up at the ski hill and the Trickle Creek Lodge that the Carlson family owned.

Craig's little girl, Meri, was the flower girl, pulling their baby girl, Julia, in a flower-covered wagon up the aisle to where the groom waited with his brothers, Asher and Chase, along with his best friend, Andy, as his groomsmen.

Craig's sisters, Charli and Kat, along with Lucy's best friend from Vancouver were Lucy's bridesmaids, filling out the bridal party.

They all looked fantastic, but not nearly as gorgeous as my wife.

Avery wore a dress that should have come with some kind of warning label on it.

It wasn't the pink and purple flowers printed on it that were the problem, although the color did make her eyes even brighter and complemented her hair, somehow making her look even more stunning.

It was the way the light, flowy fabric simultaneously hugged her curves and floated around her bare legs that stirred up a million different thoughts, each of them more R-rated than the last. And certainly not appropriate for a family-friendly event.

What I wanted to do was whisk my wife away and do some more *practicing*.

The taste of Avery's lips consumed every one of my waking thoughts. And since our first *practice* kiss on the porch, I'd found at least a half dozen other opportunities for more practicing.

After all, she said it herself...practice makes perfect. And if we were going to convince the entire town of Trickle Creek, all of whom were in attendance at the wedding, we needed to look like the real deal.

Based on how things had been going so far, I guessed we were doing a pretty good job. But it was still early.

Even so, we should have done more practicing.

Not that it would ever be enough, as far as I was concerned.

Every single time I had Avery in my arms and my lips on hers, I totally forgot that we weren't really a couple. It was to be expected, because, *damn*...just looking at my wife had my cock rock hard, never mind kissing her.

But my brain...well, that was a different story.

Holding her close, inhaling her sweet scent that was always mingled with the faintest traces of paint these days, did something to all reasonable thought.

And it wasn't just kissing and holding her—although that was pretty fucking amazing—it was just *being* with her.

It had been almost three weeks since I moved in, and we started working side by side every day. It was a little strange at first, but now, every morning, I looked forward to getting downstairs and having a coffee with Avery before starting our day together.

In my whole life, I'd never spent so much time with one person and not only not gotten tired of her, but I looked forward to spending even more time together.

A lot more time. Time that could involve—

Avery's small hand squeezing mine pulled me from my thoughts, and just in time, too, because they were about to go into very X-rated territory.

"Are you crying?" I took a second glance at Avery, who dabbed at her eyes with a tissue. "But this is supposed to be happy."

She sniffled and tried to smile. "I know, it's just…" She shrugged and turned her attention back to the couple who had just been pronounced husband and wife and were about to seal it with a kiss.

The crowd erupted in a cheer, but my eyes were on my wife. She was smiling now, but the tears fell unchecked down her cheeks.

Maybe it was just the usual emotion that weddings seemed to bring out in people—women mostly—but it felt like something more.

"Hey." I used my thumb to wipe away a tear and let my

hand linger on her cheek. When she looked at me, I leaned in and whispered, "Our kiss was better."

She burst out laughing and immediately clapped a hand over her mouth.

"It's true." I winked at her, satisfied that I'd brought the bright smile back to her face.

Avery slipped her arm through mine and leaned her head against my shoulder as we waited for the wedding party to finish signing the papers. I dropped a kiss on the top of her head and when I looked up, my eyes met Grayson's, who sat a few seats away.

He was watching us with an unreadable expression on his face. We'd always been able to read each other pretty well, but lately, I couldn't figure him out. At least, not when it came to Avery.

Probably because I was a lying piece of shit when it came to Avery and the truth. It was for a good reason, but that didn't make me feel any better about lying to my twin.

I gave Grayson a nod, at the exact moment he gave me one. We both laughed.

And then the music changed; the happy couple was officially announced and we were all on our feet, cheering the newlyweds down the aisle.

"We did it." Avery looked up at me, her eyes still shining from tears.

"Oh, sweetheart." I leaned in to steal another kiss. I kept this one as chaste as I could. "That was the warm-up," I whispered in her ear. "This party is just getting started."

Avery

I twirled the stem of my champagne glass between my fingers, my heels clicking softly against the wooden floorboards as I moved toward the dessert table. The smell of vanilla frosting and freshly baked cake had been calling me all night. I'd resisted long enough; it was almost time to succumb to my cravings.

It wasn't that I needed to justify myself, but I definitely deserved something sweet after the last few hours. Pretending to be Reid's wife wasn't stressful; I was actually starting to really like that part of things, especially the kissing. It was more that it felt like everyone was watching me, and I wasn't used to being on public display.

I sipped my champagne, letting the bubbles tickle my nose as I scanned the beautifully decorated room. The wedding was being held up at the lodge, which was a stunning log building, with stone floors and a showstopping floor-to-ceiling rock fireplace.

Every single detail had been considered. The flowers were all locally grown by the groom's sister, Charli. Dalias, snapdragons, lilies and irises and blooms I couldn't name filled vases on every single surface.

Craig, Lucy, and their girls were a beautiful family. The love in the air was palpable, and it truly was a gorgeous wedding and everything I'd imagined a wedding reception should be—intimate yet festive, full of love and laughter. The kind of wedding I once thought I might have.

The thought slipped in uninvited, and I pushed it out of my mind as I turned back toward the cluster of townsfolk chatting near the dessert table. I'd met more people tonight than I could count—neighbors, business owners, even a retired teacher who swore she'd taught Reid to read.

Everyone was kind, welcoming, and eager to share stories about the town.

Through all of it, Reid had been by my side, his arm around my waist, holding me close. Now, he lingered near a wooden pole that had been carved from what had to have once been a giant tree. His broad shoulders filled out his suit like it had been custom-made for him. His dark hair, that had been combed so neatly earlier, was a little mussed now, but it wasn't his hair I was focused on.

It was the way he watched me when he thought I wasn't looking that made my stomach flip a little.

The dessert table forgotten, I stared across the room at my husband.

The memory of his lips on mine triggered a soft ache low in my belly. We'd spent the last two days *practicing*, and it had obviously paid off with all the kissing we'd already done tonight. If anyone had any doubts about our marriage, we'd surely erased them from their thoughts.

Heck, it was getting hard for me to remember that it wasn't real. With every touch we shared, every little glance, the line between real and pretend melted a little more. It started to feel a whole lot less like acting and more like… something else entirely.

Reid was kind and steady, and the more I got to know him, the more I liked him. Even his gruffness was endearing. It helped that Grayson was right—Reid's grouchiness was really just a crunchy shell that revealed a gooey interior.

I glanced down at the simple band on my left hand. It wasn't fancy and there was nothing romantic about it or the matching one on Reid's hand. I'd ordered them online with overnight shipping when I realized people would ask. It couldn't have been more different than the big, flashy solitaire I'd once worn on that hand.

Not that I wanted it—or the man who gave it to me —back.

Still. It gave me pause to think about how things could have been different.

Shaking the thought away, I abandoned the dessert table and made my way across the room to Reid, smiling and nodding politely at the guests. It wasn't time to dwell on the past. It was time to focus on the present—on my very handsome husband, who still hadn't taken his eyes off me.

He extended an arm for me when I got close, and his eyes softened in a way that made my breath catch. "You looked deep in thought over there." He kept his voice low as he pulled me close. "Everything okay?"

"Everything is fine." It wasn't a total lie. "I'm just taking it all in."

Reid turned me a little so he could look me in the eye. "Are you sure? You seem a little—"

"I'm fine." I smiled until he nodded. "Everyone has been so friendly and welcoming. It's been a beautiful night. Let's just enjoy it."

He still didn't look convinced, but after a moment, he nodded again and took a step backward toward the dance floor. "Dance with me."

Reid

Avery's laugh drifted up to my ears as I spun her gently around the floor. Even in the dim light, her eyes sparkled up at me. She looked happy—genuinely happy—and I didn't know how to feel about the way that hit me in the gut.

She deserved to be happy.

And I couldn't deny that I loved being the man who could put that smile on her face.

I rested my other hand lightly on her waist, feeling the soft fabric of her dress against my palm. Her head tipped back to meet my gaze, her lips curved in a smile that made my chest tighten. The room seemed to shrink until it was just the two of us, the sway of her body in time with mine, the warmth of her so close.

None of this was supposed to be real. But every single thing about having Avery in my arms felt like the most real thing I'd ever had.

"What are you thinking?"

Her question caught me off guard. "What makes you think I'm thinking anything at all?"

She shook her head a little. "You have the look of a man who's thinking about something."

"Busted." There was no way I could tell her what I was really thinking. That I wished—even for a minute—that even a small part of this was real. "I was just thinking that you're the most beautiful woman in the room tonight."

"Reid!" She pretended to look horrified. "The bride is *always* the most beautiful woman on her wedding day. *Always.*"

All I could do was shrug. "It's not my fault my wife is stunning."

The smile on her face, coupled with the flush on her cheeks, melted me.

"It's true." Taking full advantage of the fact that at least one person was probably watching us, I bent as I lifted her chin and kissed those soft, delicious lips.

One thing was for sure. The greatest perk of being married to Avery—fake or not—was kissing her. I was never going to get tired of the way she tasted. Or the way a sigh slipped from her every time my tongue met hers. Or the way she pressed her body against mine and tilted her head just so to deepen our kiss.

The music transitioned to something faster, but neither of us moved. I didn't care if the earth opened beneath my feet, as long as Avery's lips were on mine.

I don't know how long we stood there in the middle of the dance floor, lost in each other. We only came apart when an enthusiastic dancer nearby bumped into me, forcing me to take a step back.

But my eyes were still pinned on her and the way her breath came a little faster, the part of her lips, slightly swollen from our kiss, and the flush on her cheeks that had deepened in the last few minutes.

"Avery." My voice was rougher than I intended.

"Yes?" Her voice was little more than a whisper, despite the loud music that pulsed around us.

My hand slid down her side, resting on the soft swell of her hip, as my thumb brushed the fabric of her dress. "This...this is starting to feel..." I trailed off, not certain I should finish the thought.

"Real." She swallowed hard, her eyes never leaving mine.

"Real," I repeated. "Very fucking real." Real wasn't even close to what this was starting to feel like.

"Maybe we should…"

"Go," I finished for her. "Yes. I definitely think we should get out of here."

The desire that flared in her eyes was all I needed to see to know that she was on exactly the same page as me.

I took her hand in mine and led her through the crowd toward the door. With any luck, we could slip away without anyone noticing. The party was in full swing, and we'd done our duty all night. Poor Avery had been introduced to almost everyone in town. From my high school science teacher to Larissa Clark, who couldn't wait to tell my new wife that we used to date.

Of course, Larissa and I had *very* different meanings of the word *date*, which was the whole reason I'd broken off our friends-with-benefits situation after only a few months. But the flash of jealousy on Avery's face was an unexpected surprise.

We managed to make it to the front steps of the lodge before we were stopped.

"You two didn't think you could sneak away without saying goodbye, did you?"

I froze, and Avery squeezed my hand before she spun around to face the source of the voice.

"Brody." It made me happy to hear the comfortable way she addressed my brother after only just officially meeting him. "You caught us." She lifted her shoulders in an innocent shrug and turned her attention to my brother's companion, Lauren Westfield.

I wasn't surprised to see the two of them together, not

really. Despite asking dozens of times, no one could ever get a straight answer out of Brody about what the situation between the two of them was. One minute, they were acting like a couple; the next, one of them was dating someone else entirely. We'd all given up trying to figure it out.

I shot my brother a pointed look, which he ignored.

"The party's just getting started."

Avery sighed and pretended to look disappointed. "It's been great," she said. "And I'd love to spend more time with you all, but we have a long day ahead of us tomorrow."

I nodded, even though we'd discussed taking the day off of any actual renovation work.

"Besides…" I pulled Avery close and rested my hand on her hip. "I am desperate to get my beautiful wife alone."

She tensed a little, but only for a second before she relaxed and added, "After all, we *are* still in our own honeymoon period." She looked up at me with a wink and a flash in her eyes that had my dick hard as a rock with the promise I saw in her gaze.

It took all the self-control I had, and even some I didn't know I was capable of, to keep from pressing her up against the wall right then and there, onlookers be dammed.

I may have broken down and done it, too, if Brody hadn't chuckled and broken the spell my wife had cast over me. "Well, we probably shouldn't keep you then."

Reluctantly, and because it was the only way to move on and get my woman home, I tore my gaze away from her and said goodbye to my brother and Lauren.

"I hope to see you soon, Avery. I look forward to learning more about you," Brody called after us, but I was already halfway back to the truck by the time his words reached us.

Nothing else was going to stop me from getting Avery home because I, too, was looking forward to learning more about my new wife.

Specifically, what her pretty face would look like when I buried myself deep inside her sweet pussy and made her come.

Chapter Nineteen

Avery

THE DOOR CLICKED SHUT behind us, the sound echoing in the quiet of the empty inn. My heart pounded so loudly I was sure Reid could hear it, but when I turned to face him, his eyes were already locked on mine.

The air between us was charged. The unspoken tension we'd danced around all night—or, more specifically, for the past few weeks—was now impossible to ignore.

He stepped closer, his hand brushing mine, and I forgot how to breathe. This wasn't part of the plan—none of this was—but right now, I couldn't bring myself to care.

"Finally," he murmured, his voice low and rough, making my pulse skip.

My palms slid up his chest, lingering over the firm muscles beneath his shirt. "Are we doing this?"

His mouth curved into a dangerous grin that sent a shot of desire straight between my legs. "Fuck, I hope so, Avery."

His fingers tightened on my waist. "Because it is long past time we consummate this marriage, don't you think?"

"Mmm." I exhaled slowly. "Definitely."

And then he kissed me.

It wasn't tentative or slow. It wasn't for practice or for the benefit of anyone who might be watching.

This kiss was just for us. It was the kind of kiss that left no room for doubt, all heat and intent, his hands framing my face like I might slip away if he released me. But I wasn't going anywhere. Not a chance.

My body was on fire. It had been way too long since I'd been kissed like that. Had I *ever* been kissed like that?

A sigh slipped from my lips as Reid's hands moved up my back to the zipper of my dress. His fingers lingered and teased over the zipper while his kisses moved from my lips to the sensitive spot just behind my ear. He kissed and sucked until I was groaning.

A loud knock on the door behind me shattered the moment. I stumbled backward, but Reid caught me before I could trip.

"What…who? Are you expecting someone?"

I shook my head. The very few people I knew in town were likely still at the wedding.

The knock sounded again. Sharper this time. "Avery. I know you're in there. I saw a vehicle."

Shit.

Reid's gaze snapped to mine, his eyes dark with an unasked question.

I took a step away from him and did my best to straighten my dress and smooth my hair. "It's Jacob."

"Who the fuck is Jacob?" Reid's nostrils flared. His fists

clenched at his side as he glared at the door, clearly ready for a fight. "You didn't tell me you had—"

"He's my cousin." I put my hand on Reid's arm and squeezed. "I don't *have* anyone."

I waited until Reid looked at me again and I could see the realization in his eyes as he understood. I couldn't help the small smile that crossed my lips, knowing he was jealous, even for a second. But the smile was short-lived when another knock reminded me of the bigger problem waiting on the porch.

"Why is your cousin here?"

"He's mad." I glanced at the door and back at my husband. "I told you he was going to contest the will."

Reid nodded.

I had told him some of the details, leaving out a few—like my cousin's actual name—and the fact that ever since the news of our wedding had reached him, he'd been blowing up my phone, threatening to prove that I was a liar. "He's still challenging our grandfather's will," I told Reid in a whisper. "He doesn't believe that our marriage is real."

"What? Why didn't you—"

"I don't really think this is the time, do you?"

He closed his mouth and pressed his lips together before giving me a curt nod. "Want me to get rid of him?"

It was tempting. Very tempting. But it wasn't going to solve the problem.

"No. Let me see what he wants." He didn't look convinced as I moved past him to the door, opening it to reveal my cousin on the porch.

I don't know why I expected it to be any different, but Jacob looked just the same as last time I'd seen him, at the funeral. Smug and self-satisfied. He'd always considered himself to be better than me, and judging by the smirk on his face, that hadn't changed in our years apart.

"It's about—"

"Can I help you with something, Jacob?" I stopped him before he could berate me for not answering the door quickly enough for him.

"Are you going to let me in?"

It was the last thing I wanted to do. "It's late. You should probably—"

"We need to talk." His eyes darted to Reid as he joined me in the doorway. I watched his eyes widen for a moment before he focused on me once more. "About our grandparents' will." He softened his voice a little, but I saw right through it. I knew he was trying to come off as caring and concerned, or even that he gave a shit that both of our grandparents were gone now.

It was bullshit. All of it.

"We can talk in the morning, Jacob. Like I said, it's late and I—"

"I've been waiting," he interrupted. "I got here hours ago but no one was here. That's not the way to run an inn."

Was he serious right now? He had to know we weren't actually open for business. If the *No Vacancy* sign hanging off the porch wasn't convincing enough, the piles of construction materials behind me and the ever-present smells of sawdust and paint should have been enough. "We're not open yet, Jacob. You know that." I didn't even try to keep the exasperation from my voice. "We were out at a—"

"It really doesn't matter where we were," Reid interrupted. He moved closer to me until we stood side by side, blocking the door completely. "Avery's right," he continued. "It's late. Why don't you come back in the morning, and we can talk properly."

"We?" Jacob raised his eyebrows and gave Reid a sidelong glance. "This is between my cousin and me."

"Avery is my *wife*." Reid emphasized the word, and it sent a tingle down my spine. "In case you didn't get the wedding announcement."

I almost laughed. Almost.

Jacob made a snorting noise, shifted his body a little and stared directly at me. "I have nowhere to stay," he said. "And this *is* still a family house until this is settled."

That wasn't entirely true, but he did have a point. No matter what I thought about Jacob, he *was* my cousin, and my grandparents would be horrified if I turned him away.

Reid moved to step forward, but I put my arm out to stop him. "It's okay," I said to my husband. "Jacob *is* family." To my cousin, I said, "You can stay."

Reid looked like he was going to argue, but I gave him a look that I hoped he understood. It wasn't worth fighting about tonight. Jacob was infuriating, to be sure. But I had a lifetime of dealing with my cousin, and aggravating him further wasn't going to help this situation. Besides, I knew exactly why he was here.

No doubt, he was coming to check on my marriage to Reid for himself. We'd already had some practice perfecting our act as a married couple at the wedding all day. It looked like that was just the dress rehearsal.

It was time for the main event.

I took Reid's hand and squeezed as we took a step back and let Jacob in.

Chapter Twenty

Reid

THIS GUY NEEDED to get the fuck out of the inn. His very presence was infuriating and putting me on edge. Never mind the evening he'd just interrupted. But there was nothing I could do about it. Not now.

Not when Avery had invited him in.

It wasn't my place to kick him out. No matter how badly I wanted to.

Still, all she had to do was say the word, and I'd haul his city boy, slick ass out to the curb and leave him there.

"We're not really set up for guests," Avery told Jacob, as if it wasn't already completely obvious. "We don't have a proper bed for you." She shot me a look when Jacob's back was turned, and I nodded in understanding.

"Why don't you make your cousin a cup of tea," I offered. "I'll see what I can do about getting a room set up for him."

More like, I'd race up the stairs and pack up all my shit

before he could see that we'd been sleeping in separate rooms. Details.

"Do you have anything stronger than tea?"

I watched Avery force a smile and nod as she led him into the kitchen. "I'm sure we can find something."

It wasn't often that I saw anything but a genuine smile on Avery's face. It was easy to spot the difference if you were paying attention. And when it came to Avery, I was always paying attention. Her cousin didn't seem to notice, which only led me to believe he didn't know her very well.

The minute they'd disappeared into the kitchen, I took the steps two at a time. This asshole was here to make trouble for Avery. Even if I didn't know all the details, I knew that much.

It didn't take a family therapist to see there was no love lost between the two of them. He was going to be looking for any loophole he could find to take this inn away from Avery, and I'd be damned if that was going to happen.

There wasn't much in my room beyond an air mattress and an old chest of drawers I'd cleaned out for the T-shirts and jeans I wore daily. I stuffed everything I could into my duffel bag before doing a sweep of the small bathroom.

Avery hadn't been exaggerating when she said we weren't set up for guests. I'd been using a sleeping bag. And if Jacob thought he was getting a freshly made bed with crisp linens and a fluffy duvet, he was mistaken.

I gave the sleeping bag a shake to "freshen it up" and dumped it on the bed in a heap.

With one last look around the room, I was confident I hadn't left any traces of myself in the room and was just about to head down the stairs when I stopped.

Avery's room—the owner's suite—was downstairs, just off the kitchen. If I waltzed down the stairs with my duffel bag of things over my shoulder, it would raise eyebrows. But I couldn't leave it upstairs.

"Shit."

This guy was proving to be a bigger pain in my ass by the second.

Out of options, I went to the end of the hall, pulled up the window, and dropped my bag into the overgrown shrubs below. No doubt, I'd scratch the hell out of my arms later retrieving it, but I had little choice.

Our *guest* was sipping a glass of whiskey when I returned to the kitchen. Avery shot me a questioning glance behind his back. I gave her a slight nod that I hoped was at least a little bit reassuring. She looked exhausted. But it was more than just being tired.

She was worried. And working hard not to let it show.

"Your room's all ready for you." I bumped his shoulder, splashing whiskey on his dress shirt as I moved past him. "Like Avery said, we're not set up for guests yet. Hope you'll be okay with a sleeping bag on an old air mattress."

I actually hoped he wouldn't be okay with it. And it only just occurred to me that I should have popped a hole in the mattress so the jackass ended up on the floor.

Missed opportunity.

"It'll do." Jacob narrowed his eyes in my direction as I slipped my arm around Avery's waist and pulled her close so she could rest her head on my shoulder. "So, you two." He gestured between us with his glass before taking a sip, like a total douche. "How did you say you met again?"

"I don't think we did," I answered quickly, saving Avery from a conversation she didn't want to have.

Jacob snorted, and Avery squeezed my arm a little. "We actually met years ago when we were kids and I'd spend my summers here with Grandma and Grandpa."

It wasn't something we'd discussed again. Even if neither of us remembered it well, it was still the truth.

"I always felt like there was something between us back then, but it wasn't until I ran into Reid at the hardware store when I first arrived that the little spark that had been lit all those years ago really lit into a fire, isn't that right?"

I looked down into her eyes, which once again sparkled with life. If it was a little storytelling that had brought that spark back, I was more than happy to play along.

"That's right, sweetheart." I held her gaze for a moment before reluctantly looking at her cousin. "The moment I heard her voice in the hardware store, my heart knew exactly what it wanted. What it had wanted since we were too young to understand what it was."

Okay, I was playing it up a little. But what the hell.

"It was like love at first sight, wasn't it, sweetheart?"

Avery shook her head with a little grin. "Absolutely. Only it wasn't first sight."

"Right." Jacob drew out the word with an eye roll. "Because you two had some sort of romance when you were *children*?" Disbelief dripped from his words, but I was not to be deterred.

"Obviously, we were too young and stupid to know what those feelings meant back then." I spoke directly to Avery. "But the moment our eyes locked, I felt it. And when I gave you that boost through the window when you couldn't get in the front door…well, that was it for me."

Her lips quirked up into the beginning of a smile. She was enjoying this, and she wasn't the only one.

"When did you know I was the one for you, sweetheart?"

She shocked me, by not even thinking about it. "Easy." She looked me straight in the eye. "When I saw you in the ice cream store with your niece. You were laughing and your eyes crinkled up in the corners at whatever she was telling you. I could see how much you loved her and…well…" She shrugged, but didn't look away as she added, "I fell head over heels and in that moment, I knew you were the man for me. Forever."

Fuck.

Me.

This wasn't real. I knew it wasn't. We were putting on a show. We were making it believable.

But Avery just blew right past pretend and straight into very, *very* real.

There was only one reaction to that. Audience or not, I held my wife's cheeks in my hands, tipped my head down to meet hers, and gave her a very real kiss.

Chapter Twenty-One

Avery

IT HAD BEEN A LONG DAY. A very long day. The wedding and being on the dance floor in Reid's arms felt like it had happened a lifetime ago. All I wanted to do was crawl under the covers, put my head on the pillow, and sleep away the stress currently creeping up my spine.

I knew Jacob was going to be a problem. Maybe it was naive of me, but I didn't really expect him to come to Trickle Creek and challenge me in person. My cousin was more of a *hide-behind-a-lawyer* type.

Having him here was definitely going to complicate things. Not the least of which were my feelings for Reid, which were growing and changing and...well, becoming more and more complicated all the time.

I spun, a pillow in my hand when the bedroom door clicked open and he appeared. "I made sure to lock the door."

"You did? But I thought you said no one locked their doors in Trickle Creek?"

"They don't." He leaned against the closed door. "But *you* do. So I locked it for you."

My heart did a weird flippy thing, and my feelings twisted up into the next level of *complicated.*

"Thank you."

He shrugged and for the first time, I noticed he had leaves in his hair, and his dress shirt was dirty and untucked. And were those scratches on his arms?

"What on earth happened while you were locking up?"

Reid shook his head and held out a duffel bag. "I threw it out the window earlier and it landed in rosebushes."

"Oh." I tried to stifle the giggle with my hand, but it didn't work. I crossed the room and took the bag from him, giving his arms a once-over. The scratches didn't look too bad. "I didn't think of that. Thanks for doing that." I let my fingers linger on his skin. "Thanks for all of this. I didn't expect Jacob to just…"

"Were you going to tell me what a problem he was being?"

Suddenly exhausted, I left him standing by the door and moved toward the bed. "I was hoping I could handle it. I sent him a copy of our marriage certificate and that should have been enough."

"But it wasn't."

I shook my head, flipped the blankets back, and crawled into bed.

Without another word, and with an expression I couldn't read on his face, Reid took his duffel and moved past me to the attached bathroom.

The stress from the last few hours seeped from my pores, and for the first time, I wondered whether we were going to be able to pull this off. I had no idea how long Jacob planned to stay or what his agenda was beyond making my life difficult.

That wasn't entirely true. I knew exactly what his agenda was. He wanted to prove my marriage to Reid wasn't real so he could challenge my right to the inn. My lawyer had already warned me that if I was found to be in violation of the terms, the will would be null and void, and the inn would be put up for sale. Considering I didn't have any money besides the small amount that was part of my inheritance—that I'd also lose—I wouldn't be able to buy it.

Not only that, but all the money that I'd put on credit to start the renovation while we waited would come due and I'd have no way to pay the debt.

It had been a risk. A big one. I knew it at the time, but I did it anyway because I'd been so sure it would all work out okay.

Now...I was having doubts.

I pinched the bridge of my nose and dropped my head back against the headboard, willing the headache that was rapidly forming to go away.

"You should have told me."

My eyes snapped open to see Reid standing in the bathroom door with nothing on but a pair of boxer shorts.

"What are you...what...did you..." I tripped over my words, unable to form a coherent thought as my eyes raked over his bare chest.

I knew he was strong. I felt those muscles when we danced and when he wrapped his arms around me to hold me close while he kissed me. But *knowing* was different than *seeing.* And I was seeing a lot.

"Do you have a headache?" He stepped closer, his face a mask of concern.

"What?"

"You were pinching your…"

Reid touched the bridge of my nose so gently, I closed my eyes again and took a deep breath.

"Yes." I nodded. "A little bit. It's just been…" I blew out a breath. "Well, it's been a lot today."

"It has." He smoothed his fingers over my forehead and down my cheek. "And it's not over yet, because…" He shrugged and looked to the other side of the bed.

"Oh." It was only then that I realized that, of course, Reid was going to be sleeping in my bed with me. Logically, I knew that with Jacob here and in Reid's bedroom, there weren't any other options. But somehow my brain hadn't made the connection of what exactly that meant.

Or that it was only a few hours ago when my bed was exactly where we were headed.

"Don't worry." He moved around to the other side of the bed and pulled the covers back. "I promise to be a perfect gentleman."

I knew he would. Even if I didn't want him to be. And if I wasn't so emotionally wrung out, I definitely wouldn't want him to be.

The mattress sunk under his weight, and I braced myself a little to keep from rolling into him.

"Unless, of course, you don't want me to be."

For a moment, I considered the stress relief that Reid

would no doubt be able to provide, but ultimately it wasn't right.

"I don't think it's a matter of me wanting it or not." We were lying so close I could feel his hot, pepperminty breath on my cheek.

Reid shifted beside me, the movement slow and deliberate, as if he were giving me time to adjust to his presence. His arm brushed mine, sending a spark of awareness racing through me.

"I get it," he said after a moment. "You don't have to explain yourself."

But that was the problem—I *wanted* to explain myself. I wanted to at least try to explain the tornado of feelings that I couldn't quite name, the pull toward him that grew in intensity by the second. I wanted him to understand how hard it was trying to remember that this thing between us wasn't real.

I *needed* him to know that my hesitancy wasn't about him or even about me; it was about trying to make sense of everything that was happening.

"You're overthinking." His voice cut through the haze of my thoughts.

"You don't know that."

He smiled, just a little. It was an expression I was seeing more and more from him. I liked it. More than that, I liked that he seemed to reserve it just for me.

"Sure I do. It's written all over your face. You're lying here, worrying about everything except what it is you really want."

"What I want doesn't matter right now."

"Doesn't it?" His gaze dropped to my lips.

My breath caught.

I couldn't answer. My heart beat too fast, and my thoughts were too jumbled. Instead, I did the only thing I could think of—I closed my eyes, hoping the darkness would give me some clarity.

The silence stretched between us, heavy and charged. I felt the heat radiating from his body, the way he was holding himself back. It would be so easy to close the distance and give in to this thing between us.

But instead of moving closer, he whispered, "Goodnight, Avery."

I opened my eyes to find him already turned on his side, his back to me. The tension in the air eased, but it left something raw and aching in its place.

"Goodnight."

I turned to my side, too, and stared at the wall, waiting for sleep to pull me under. But even as I felt myself drift off, I couldn't quite shake the lingering warmth of him beside me—or the quiet certainty that this wasn't the end of whatever this was between us.

Chapter Twenty-Two

Reid

THE KITCHEN WAS TOO small for three people, especially when one of them was Avery's unwelcome cousin, Jacob. I lingered in the doorway for a moment, freshly showered, but nowhere near relaxed or ready to face whatever it was this asshole wanted.

Spending the night in Avery's bed was...well, it was equal parts amazing and torturous. At some point, I rolled over and wrapped my arm around her. I'd woken up to the scent of her hair and the warmth of her pressed up against my body. My dick was rock hard and aching, and ultimately what drove me from the bed before dawn.

I'd spent longer than I should have in the shower, but dammit, I'd needed that extra time with thoughts of Avery and my right hand. There was no way I was going to be able to navigate another day pretending to be something I wasn't, but more and more wanted to be.

I watched Avery now, moving about the kitchen, shifting

her attention between the bacon on the stove and her cousin sitting at the table.

She was working hard to appear casual, but I could see the tension in her shoulders. The way her brow was furrowed just a little bit and how forced her usually easy, bright smile was.

And the smug son of a bitch, lounging in the chair with his arms crossed behind his head, was the reason for all of it.

The cocky grin on his face set my teeth on edge.

I didn't know his story. But I didn't need to know the details to know that whatever it was he wanted, it wasn't good. If he was looking for a hole in our story, I sure as hell wasn't going to give it to him.

"Good morning." I crossed the short distance to my wife at the stove and pulled her into my arms for a deep and completely inappropriate kiss. "You slipped away before I could wake you up properly, sweetheart."

Avery sucked in a breath but before she could say anything, I kissed her again. This time, I slipped my tongue between her lips, pulling a sweet groan from her that hit a spot deep in my belly. My hands slid down her sides, to her hips.

Without taking my mouth off hers, I lifted her easily and set her on the counter. Her arms wrapped around my neck, pulling me closer as I shifted my body between her legs.

I was so lost in her, that I'd almost forgotten the entire reason for the kiss in the first place.

Behind me, Jacob cleared his throat loudly. "Bacon's going to burn."

"Oh!" Avery pulled back, and I instantly missed her lips on mine.

From Grumpy to Forever

So much for trying to get my raging desire for this woman under control. My dick was once again fully awake.

I took the opportunity to give her one more kiss before stepping back and turning my attention to the bacon—which was not, in fact, going to burn—on the stove.

"Sorry, man," I said over my shoulder. "Forgot you were here."

"Uh-huh."

I grinned to myself. Hell, maybe I was going to like this little game after all. Pretending to be Avery's husband, first at the wedding and now, right here at home, definitely had perks. A whole lot of perks.

Avery had recovered from my unexpected greeting and had hopped off the counter. "Coffee, Reid?"

"Thank you, sweetheart." I turned to take the cup from her and gave her another kiss. "I just can't keep my hands off her," I said to Jacob. "You know how it is, right? When you find that person you just can't stay away from."

Judging by the look on his face, Jacob did not know what it was like. I leaned up against the counter and sipped my coffee for a few minutes, letting the silence grow.

After a few minutes, Avery moved past me with a platter of toast and bacon. "Breakfast is ready." She set the food on the table and looked at me expectantly.

The last thing I wanted to do was leave Avery alone with this asshole, but I had a busy day ahead of me. Besides, I knew she'd be able to hold her own. "I'll take mine to go, sweetheart." I gave her an apologetic smile. "I promised Grayson I'd be at the store first thing to pick up our lumber order. And then I'm going to head over to the shop and get a few things set up there this afternoon. I was hoping to take you over and…"

"Sorry." Her lips dipped down, but I stopped her before it could turn into a frown.

"It's not your fault." I winked at her. "Unexpected houseguests are just that—*unexpected.*" I moved to the table and built myself a breakfast sandwich with two pieces of toast, some bacon, and a fried egg from the plate. "How long are you planning to stay, Jake?"

"It's Jacob."

"Whatever." I shrugged and took a bite of my sandwich. "The airbed can't possibly be very comfortable."

Truthfully, it wasn't terrible. But compared to the warm coziness of Avery's bed, it might as well have been a slab of concrete.

"It'll do," Jacob said. "For now. But we're going to have to order some guest beds if we plan on—"

"*We* don't plan on anything." The spatula still in her hand, Avery crossed her arms and glared at her cousin.

Oh yes, she'd be able to handle herself just fine.

"Reid and I have a plan to finish the renovations and get ready for a grand opening," she continued. "You don't need to concern yourself with any of it, Jacob, because the inn is mine and not yours."

"For now."

"No." She jabbed the spatula in his direction. "Forever."

My phone vibrated in my pocket. It was Grayson. Shit. The order had arrived early.

"Sweetheart, I'm sorry." I held up my phone. "I can tell him—"

"No. Go. I've got this."

I gave her a questioning look that I hoped told her I would change every one of my plans if she needed me to.

"Really, Reid. I can handle this." She waved the spatula, which was starting to look like a weapon. "Besides, there's nothing to handle. The inn is legally mine whether he likes it or not. Jacob probably just wanted to come to see it one last time before he accepted that as fact. Isn't that right, cousin?"

Damn, Avery was good. She knew what buttons to push, and she'd done it with that sweet smile on her face.

He was trying to stay calm, but Jacob's face was red when he finally sat back in his chair. "Not at all, *cuz*. There is no way in hell that you met and married a total stranger in under three weeks. And I'm here to prove it. This marriage is a total sham. Which means that you are in violation of the terms of the will. And the inn will be going up for sale by the end of the week."

My hands clenched into fists at my sides, and I took a step toward the asshole, before Avery's hand on my chest stopped me.

"Go." She gave me a look. "I'll see you later."

I hated leaving her with him. Hell, I hated leaving her at all. A truth that was getting harder and harder to deny. But she was right. It would be better for everyone if I got some space.

For now.

Chapter Twenty-Three

Avery

THE PILE of weeds next to me was getting bigger, but the gardens didn't look any more under control than they had when I started.

Still, digging in the dirt and yanking out weeds and over-grown shrubs was exactly the type of therapy I needed. At least, it should have been.

When Jacob decided to walk into town and spend the morning "exploring the town," which I was certain was only code for "try to dig up dirt on me and my marriage to Reid," I jumped at the opportunity to clear my head and get some work done.

The gardening should have been just the relaxing and mind-numbing work I needed to get some type of clarity because what I really needed was to figure out how to get Jacob to back off so everything could move forward the way it was supposed to.

My bills were piling up. A detail I hadn't shared with

Reid yet. Truthfully, it wouldn't be a problem if I could just get the judge to sign off on the will and make the inn—and the inheritance I needed to pay for the renovations—official.

But if the judge didn't sign off…I couldn't let myself think of the complete and total personal ruin it would mean.

I stabbed the trowel in the dirt again as if it had personally offended me and dug around the base of a particularly stubborn weed.

Yes. I *should* be coming up with a solution for what to do about Jacob. But the only thing I could think of was Reid.

And the way we'd kissed last night. The way he'd touched me. The way he'd looked at me like he couldn't go another second without having me.

Heat crept up my neck as I remembered how close I'd come to making a huge mistake—*or maybe the best decision of my life.*

No.

It wasn't going to do any good to think about how we'd almost crossed the line of our fake marriage in every single way. And how I wished we had.

I'd tossed and turned all night, thinking about what could have happened if we hadn't been interrupted.

But wasn't it a good thing that we'd been interrupted when we had? Wouldn't actually sleeping with my husband complicate the fact that our marriage was nothing more than an arrangement? Even if it felt more and more real with every passing minute.

Abandoning my trowel, I wrapped my hands around the base of the weed and tugged. It didn't budge. "Come on!" I stabbed at it again with my tool before pulling once more. It moved a little, so I stood for more leverage and put all my weight behind the stubborn weed. "Come on, you little —oof!"

I landed hard on my ass on the lawn. The weed stood proudly in the garden, mocking me.

With a grunt, I stood, dusted my shorts off and headed for the porch. What I really wanted to do was sit on the swing and forget everything. But the empty chains dangling from the porch roof where the swing should be hanging only reminded me of how much work still needed to be done.

I fought back the urge to cry in frustration and reached instead for my cell phone that I'd left on the step.

I pushed the button to call my best friend. I didn't even wait for a hello the second she picked up. "Tell me I'm not losing my mind."

She didn't miss a beat. "You know I can't tell you that." I scowled but she laughed. "What's going on?"

"Besides taking on a project I can't possibly do justice to, marrying a man I hardly know but can't keep my hands off of, and my cousin showing up out of the blue on my doorstep trying to prove it's all fake?" I blow out a breath. "Besides that, nothing."

"Whoa." It wasn't a video call, but I could picture the look on my best friend's face. "Go back. What about not being able to keep your hands off your husband? What's that all about?"

"That's what you want to hear about?" I shook my head before dropping it back and looking up to the sky. "Out of everything, you want to know about Reid?"

"You know I do." She laughed. "And something tells me that's what you really want to talk about." She wasn't wrong.

"Have you guys consummated your marriage yet?" She emphasized the word marriage, and I almost regretted having told her the truth. Almost. I needed to tell someone, and it seemed safest to confide in Carrie considering she was hours away and not likely to blow our cover.

"We haven't."

"But you want to."

Dammit. Why did she know me so well? I blew out another breath and told her the truth. "I do. I really, really do."

"So what's the issue? He's a hottie, isn't he?"

"How do you know?"

She laughed again. "I do know how to use the internet, you know. He doesn't have much of a social media presence, but I found him tagged in a few pictures. He's super hot."

He was. I didn't need to confirm it.

"So why do you sound so worked up about it?" Before I could answer, Carrie continued. "Wait. I know you. It's not just him. It's everything, right?"

I nodded despite the fact she couldn't see me. Fortunately, Carrie didn't need the confirmation.

"Okay, let's take this piece by piece."

The stress seeped out of my bones as my best friend took control of the situation in only the way a friend who knew you as well as she knew me could.

"First of all, the inn is not too big of a project for you to do justice on it. I know you, Avery, and I know how much you love that place. You're going to do your very best to make sure it's perfect. Your grandparents would have been so proud of you. And you know it."

143

I inhaled through my nose and told myself not to cry. She was right.

"Yes, you're married to a man you hardly know. But the very fact that he's willing to participate in this with you tells me he's a good guy. Besides that, you have excellent radar."

Before I could object, she jumped in again.

"Except for that brief lapse of judgment with Porter, but you got that out of your system." I didn't even bother to swallow up my laughter as she kept going. "We'll come back to the attraction part. It's important."

I could almost see her wiggling her eyebrows.

"But let's talk about your shitty cousin for a second. Because that's all the time he's worth. First of all, you have nothing to worry about. Your marriage is legal, and he's only grasping at straws here because he's butt hurt that your grandparents left the inn to you."

"But he has more money to fight than I do." I didn't bother to tell her that I was so deeply in debt with this whole situation that if it didn't get sorted soon, Jacob would be the least of my issues. "I won't be able to drag it out if that's what he decides to do."

"He won't."

She sounded so sure, I wished I had even a fraction of that confidence.

"When he sees that you and Reid are the real deal, he'll drop it. Now, let's get to the good stuff. Why are you so worked up about sleeping with the man? You're a grown-up. Just do it."

"It's not that simple."

"Sure looks that way to me. He's a hottie. You're a

hottie. And besides, Avery…did you miss the very obvious thing here?"

I lifted my shoulders in a shrug. "I must have."

"You're married to the man, Avery," Carrie said matter-of-factly. "Reid is your husband."

She punctuated every word as if I needed help understanding what she was saying. Maybe I did.

"If you both want to have sex, do it. Consummate your marriage. If anything, it only makes it more legit. Besides, you're both consenting adults. I do not see what the problem is here?"

Of course she didn't see the problem. That's because she didn't see the way Reid looked at me. The way he stood up to Jacob for me. The way he made me feel cared for and protected. The way I got butterflies every time he came close. The way my entire body vibrated when he gave me that rare smile that only I seemed to be on the receiving end of. Carrie didn't see any of that. And my best friend certainly didn't see the way I was with him or the fact that I was falling for him. Hard.

And she wouldn't see that unless I told her.

With a sigh, I started, "The problem, Carrie, is—"

"Avery!"

I jolted at the sound of my name on my cousin's lips.

Dammit.

"Shit, Carrie. Jacob's back. I need to—"

"Avery." Jacob rounded the corner, and he didn't look impressed. "I don't know what the hell you're up to here."

"Call me later," Carrie said into the phone. "Unless you're too busy with that sexy husband of yours. In that case, call me *much* later."

I hung up with a shake of my head, her laughter still ringing in my ears as I set my phone down and stood.

"How was town?" I asked lightly. "Was it everything you remembered Trickle Creek to be?"

He stopped inches from me and looked down at me in a move meant to be intimidating. I wasn't going to let him get away with it, so I stepped back and up onto the porch step, putting our eyes on level.

"I don't know what you're up to here, Avery. But I know it's something."

"I don't know what you're talking about."

He shook his head and chuckled. There was no humor in it. "I was asking around about you."

I worked hard to keep my face a blank mask. "And what did you learn?"

"I learned that I'm not the only one surprised by your sudden marriage." He crossed his arms, looking quite pleased with himself. "In fact, there was more than one person in town who had a hard time believing that Reid Lyons would settle down at all, let alone with someone he barely knew."

"Well, I guess that just goes to show how little people actually know about what's going on."

I held my position. There was no way I was going to back down. Not to Jacob. Not when so much was on the line. "I don't know what you hope to find, Jacob. But Reid and I are legally married and the inn is mine. You don't have to like it. But you do have to accept it."

His lips curled up into a sneer. "That's where you're wrong, cousin." Jacob shook his head. "I don't have to accept it. Because I know you're up to something. And if you loved this place as much as you claim to, you'd admit the truth before things get ugly."

I opened my mouth to protest but didn't have a chance before he fired off again.

"But you'll never do that, will you, Avery? You and I both know you'd rather watch this place burn than give it to me."

I sucked in a breath, but there was nothing I could say as he turned on his heel and stalked off. Because I wasn't entirely certain that he might not be right.

Chapter Twenty-Four

Reid

WITH GRAYSON ON ONE END, we hefted the final board onto the stack of wood loaded on the back of my truck. It was hot, sweaty work, especially on a warm day, but I relished it.

I needed some kind of outlet for the emotions that had been raging through me all morning. And considering punching Jacob in the face was more likely to end in me facing charges than it would him leaving town—not that I wasn't willing to make that sacrifice to see the look on his face when I decked him—lifting heavy shit was probably the best choice.

At least for now.

"What else do I need?" I wiped the sweat off my brow with the back of my arm and looked at my brother. "Anything else on Avery's list? Or can we move on to mine?"

"Yours?" My twin shook his head. "Shit, brother. I don't think you can fit much more on there."

"I'll borrow the trailer. Let's go."

Grayson shook his head and turned to walk away. "Let's take a water break. I didn't sign up for a workout this morning."

Reluctantly, I followed him into the air conditioning of the shop. "Why are you loading? Don't you have employees for this?"

He tossed me a bottle of water and popped the top on his own before answering. "It's the middle of the week. Most of my employees are still in school. Besides, I thought you might want to talk." He gave me a look before tipping the bottle to his lips.

Talk? Fuck that. I wanted to fight. Just not with Grayson.

"Nope. Nothing to talk about." I knew my brother. Just as well as he knew me. Which was why I knew it was fucking killing him not to ask all the questions that were no doubt on the tip of his tongue.

I also knew he wouldn't say a damn thing until I gave him an opening.

Which was exactly why I took my water bottle and walked to the other end of the shop, where he kept the few cuts of specialty hardwoods that he brought in. A nice piece of oak caught my eye. I ran my hand over the smooth surface and immediately I knew exactly what I'd do with such a piece.

"Add this to my tab, Gray."

"Which one? They're both growing." My brother shook his head, but he didn't say no.

"Mine." I rejoined him where he lounged in the shade. "And what do you mean, they're both growing?" I had a tab with the shop, but I paid it regularly.

"Avery's bill is getting bigger every day, man." He tipped his bottle to his lips and finished it before crunching the plastic and tossing it into a recycling bin. "I'd be worried if it was anyone else. But..."

"She's my wife."

"She's your wife," he repeated, but I didn't miss the question in his voice. "I am going to have to close it out at the end of the month, though. She said something about a payment from the estate coming in..."

He was obviously waiting for some kind of reassurance, so I swallowed my mouthful of water and pretended I knew what the hell he was talking about. "Right. That's coming in as soon as everything is settled with the lawyers."

Fucking Jacob.

This whole thing with her cousin wasn't just holding up the ownership of the inn—it was also interfering with the finances. Shit. It wasn't something I'd considered.

The asshole was putting everything in jeopardy. What I didn't know, however—and was going to ask her about as soon as I got the chance—was why she hadn't told me that so much of the project was financed on credit.

Which meant...if Jacob was successful in holding things up too much longer, Grayson was going to have to collect on the bill and...*fuck.*

Worse, if he was successful in proving that—*no*. I refused to let myself think anything of the sort. That wasn't going to happen. Because Avery and I were—well, I still didn't know what the fuck we were. But what I did know was that whatever it was, it was real.

There was nothing fake about—

"Reid!" My brother clapped his hands in front of my face. "Did you hear anything I just said?"

I scrubbed a hand over my face. "Of course. You said you needed to collect on the—"

"No. I was talking about the Sprout n' Shout. Tilley Beckett was in here earlier with a poster advertising it. Looks like it's some kind of festival focused around flowers, where people bring in plants and seeds and you can take what you...whatever. You guys are going to be there, right? It'll be a good opportunity to grab some new perennials for the inn and maybe clear out some—"

"What the fuck are you talking about?" I'd made my best effort, but I had no fucking idea what my brother was going on about. "Plant, what? Perennials for the inn? Respectfully, what the hell are you talking about, Gray?"

My brother was a patient man, but I could see I'd just about exhausted whatever reserves he might have. "You and Avery. We'll see you there, right? It'll be a good time to—"

"Right. Grab some plants for the inn and fill out the gardens," I finished for him, my brain finally catching up with the conversation. "I was listening."

I didn't miss the way he rolled his eyes. It would also be a good time for the two of us to put in another public appearance and hopefully shut Jacob up once and for all.

"Tilley mentioned that you and that beautiful wife of yours are the talk of the town."

Fuck. Of course we were.

Maybe not the whole town. But there was no doubt our names were on Tilley Beckett's tongue, that was for sure. In a way, I sort of brought it on myself by practically proposing in front of her, but that couldn't be helped now. "Well, maybe we should skip this thing then. I don't know if I need to subject Avery to any more public scrutiny."

Grayson shook his head and scratched at his chin. I could tell he was working hard to keep an opinion to himself.

"What?"

"I didn't say a word." He raised his eyebrows.

"You didn't have to."

"You want to know what I think?"

"No," I answered honestly. "I really don't. But I also don't think you're going to be able to keep it to yourself. So go ahead."

Grayson frowned and shook his head. But after a moment, he started talking, just like I knew he would. "I think that's exactly why you should both be there."

"To expose Avery to more scrutiny?"

"Yes."

My fingers twitched. If he wasn't my twin—and he didn't have a good point—I'd knock him out right now.

Reading my mind, he chuckled. "I'm not going to pretend to know what exactly you're up to, Reid. But I know you well enough to know it's something. And no." He held up a hand. "I'm not asking you to come clean. I figure if you're going to these lengths to keep it quiet, it's important. So, I'm not going to ask. But I will give you my opinion. Whether you want it or not. And that opinion is that if you want people to think you're the happily married couple that you obviously are"—a growl rumbled inside me, but again, he held up his hand and continued—"people need to see it for themselves," he finished.

"We were *just* at the wedding."

"You were." He nodded. "And everyone is talking about it. Now's the perfect time to keep them talking. In a good way. Hiding out in the inn, no matter how much you might prefer it, is not going to satisfy anyone's curiosity. And like it or not, brother, the entire town is watching you."

I let his words sink in for a moment. Reality set in as I blew out the breath I'd been holding. "Fuck."

"Exactly." Grayson didn't bother hiding his grin as he shook his head. "So I guess we'll see you there?"

I growled in his direction, grabbed my paperwork, and headed to the shop for a few hours of quiet. Maybe if I was alone, I'd be able to think this through.

There was something Avery wasn't telling me. And if she was working herself into a mountain of debt, it was crucial that we make the ownership of the inn official as soon as possible. I wasn't going to let her lose the inn. No matter what.

Even if it meant losing her.

The thought hit me like a truck as I drove away.

We were only married in name. And only so Avery could secure her inheritance. There was no other reason.

No matter what I was starting to feel.

Which meant, when her inheritance was official, there was no reason for us to continue the farce of our marriage.

And I'd lose her.

Just when I'd found her.

Chapter Twenty-Five

Avery

EVERY MUSCLE in my body ached. Even muscles I didn't know I had. What was it about gardening—or, more specifically, wrestling with weeds the size of small trees—that was so exhausting?

I let the hot water spill over my head and streak down my body in rivulets, washing the dirt and grime as well as the stress of the day down the drain.

It wasn't just a day spent in the hot sun trying to tame the garden that had drained me, and I knew it. The confrontation with Jacob had taken more out of me than I'd realized. Or maybe it was the reality of what that conversation had meant. I knew he was right. I wasn't going to let him have the inn. No matter what. But would I really let everything my grandparents loved so much be destroyed rather than let him have it?

The question had plagued me all day. Did I even deserve to have the inn if that was true?

No matter how many overgrown shrubs I'd pruned, dead plants I'd dug up, or invasive weeds I'd pulled, I still didn't have the answer to that question.

I cranked the faucet to the left until the water was steaming and almost scalding as it washed over me. The steam filled the bathroom and only belatedly did I realize I should have started the fan. But it didn't matter. If there was condensation on the paint or water damage, it was just one more thing on my list that would need to be fixed.

The thought of the ever-growing list would've made me cry if it wasn't for Reid. If I didn't have Reid, all of this would be so much harder. I don't know how or when it happened, but somewhere over the last few weeks, I'd started to rely on him for more than just fixing up the inn.

He'd become my confidant, my shoulder to cry on, and...

"Avery?" I heard my name and the knock on the door almost at the same time. "Are you in—what the...it's like a steam room in here."

"Reid? Oh. Yeah, I forgot to turn the fan on."

A moment later, I heard the flick of the switch and the creaky old fan in the ceiling started up. "Sorry," Reid said. "I didn't mean to barge in on you. I just saw the steam and I didn't want anything to—"

"It's fine." My voice shook with a surge of emotion for this man who'd known me for such a short time but cared more than some of my own flesh and blood about the inn— and me.

I wasn't the only one who noticed the waver in my voice. "Avery? Are you okay?"

Normally, I'd lie. Especially considering I was naked and

only inches away from him with nothing more than a thin plastic sheet between us. But with Reid, I didn't have to pretend. "No," I said after a moment. "I had a rough day with Jacob and…I just…"

"Can I help?"

Suddenly, my best friend's voice popped into my head. *Could he help?* Yes. If *help* meant taking my mind off my worries and stress, even for a few minutes, then *yes*, Reid could definitely help.

Besides, as Carrie had made clear to me, we *were* married, after all. Why not consummate it?

Before I could let logic or good sense get in the way, I tugged the shower curtain open to see Reid looking sexy as hell in sawdust-covered jeans and a T-shirt that strained against his chest and tightened over his biceps.

His eyes darkened as he took in the sight of me. His nostrils flared and he took a step closer.

"Yes," I said softly, my gaze locked on his. "I think you can help me very much."

Reid

Fuck yes. I could help her. I could help her very much. As long as the help she needed involved my mouth on her lips, my hands on her body, and my currently rock-hard cock buried very deeply inside her.

My shirt was off before my next breath. My hand on my belt as I took another step toward her. I didn't take my eyes off hers. Afraid if I looked away from the need in her eyes, I'd come to my senses about what I was about to do. Then again, Avery *was* my wife. We *were* consenting adults. And she *had* invited me in.

I'd be a damn fool not to get in the shower with her. And I was a lot of things, but I was absolutely *not* a fool.

Not when it came to the beautiful and very naked woman in front of me.

"Avery?" I dropped my jeans to the ground. My dick, free from its confines, stood hard and proud. I watched as her eyes dipped lower before once more meeting my eyes. "We're good?"

She bit her bottom lip, sucking it between her teeth in a way that sparked something primal deep inside me before she nodded. "Oh yes. We're good." Avery stepped aside, making room in the shower for me. "Very good. Now get in here."

"Yes, ma'am."

In a flash, I was under the spray of hot water. I took a moment to take in the magnificent sight in front of me. Damn, was she ever beautiful.

Avery was all soft curves, from her round, perfect tits to the swell of her hips and the delicious ass cheeks that had been teasing me in those cutoff shorts from the very first day I'd met her.

"Fuck, you're gorgeous." It was the only thing I could say before my lips crashed onto hers and I pushed her back against the tile wall.

She tasted even sweeter than she looked, and it wasn't long before I knew I was never going to get enough of her. A moan slipped from her lips as I deepened the kiss, twisting my tongue with hers.

Every inch of my body was pressed against her slick

skin, but I still couldn't get her close enough. Without moving my mouth from hers, I let one hand slide down her side. "You feel so good, Avery," I moaned against her mouth before once more claiming it with my own. "Every fucking part of you feels so amazing."

It took every bit of self-control I could pull together to keep from taking her right there against the shower wall, because dammit, if her body felt this good pressed up against me, being inside her would be incredible.

Forcing myself to slow down, I tore my mouth away from hers, leaving her gasping for more as I turned my attention to her neck and the sensitive spot behind her ear.

"Oh, oh." Avery arched her back and pressed her palms flat against the tile while I nibbled, kissed, and sucked her neck. "Reid, that feels so good. It's been so…yes."

Was she about to tell me how long it'd been since she'd been kissed properly? Touched the way she deserves to be touched? The thought both angered me and fueled me at the same time. Angry because this woman deserved to be worshipped and kissed like the goddess she was every single day. And that fueled me because I was more than happy to give her what she wanted. No, what she *needed*.

But it wasn't enough. It was never going to be enough with Avery. I knew that long before I set foot in the shower with her. This would only be the beginning. At least for me. Whatever this was, whatever was going on with her that led her to pull that curtain aside, I didn't care. Because for me, this was about so much more, and I had to believe she felt it, too.

Leaving her neck, I moved down her body, taking time

to lick the rivulets of water off each of her breasts, sucking first one nipple and then the next into my mouth.

I used my hands to knead her perfect mounds until she writhed with desire, thrusting her hips hungrily.

"Reid, I—"

"I know." I silenced her with a finger. "I know what you need, sweetheart. And I'm going to give it to you, I promise. But I'm going to do it my way."

"How did I know you were going to say that?"

I dropped to my knees on the tile and grinned up at her. "Because it's always my way, sweetheart. You must know that by now?"

She laughed and threaded her hands through my hair. "I just let you think that." Her wink was wicked sexy and had my cock throbbing.

But I couldn't deny it. Nor did I care to. Not when her sweet pussy was right in front of me. Oh no, I had other plans, and they involved making my wife scream as she came so hard she forgot whatever had her worked up when she got in the shower tonight.

With a hand on each thigh, I tugged them apart to give me better access.

I looked up long enough to see the look of shock on her face before I buried my face deep. Avery cried out as my tongue traveled the length of her slit before plunging between her sweet folds.

Damn. I was right. She was just as delicious as I knew she would be.

Already so wet for me, her juices coated my tongue as I took my time kissing and licking.

"Reid." My name was little more than a breath on her

ELENA AITKEN

lips as she struggled to maintain control. It was the one thing I wanted her to let go of.

"Come for me, Avery." I looked up and met her eyes. "Let go, sweetheart." With a wink, I once more bent to my task. This time, my lips locked over her sensitive bud and I suckled with just enough pressure for her to come completely undone.

Her orgasm hit hard and fast. I used one hand to brace her hip while I continued to kiss and lap up her delicious juices before getting to my feet.

I used one hand to wipe my bottom lip before kissing her long and slow. "There," I said when she could once more focus on me. "Did that help?"

Avery nodded slowly, a sly smile crossing her lips. "Definitely."

"I aim to please."

"You certainly did that." She reached out and dragged a finger down my chest, to my belly and the head of my very hard cock. I shuddered under her touch. "But I think I might need a little more help, still."

My grin matched hers, and I almost lost complete control when her fingers wrapped around my girth and squeezed. "Fuck yes. I was hoping you'd say that."

Avery

Steam clung to me as Reid backed me out of the shower, toward the bedroom. His eyes never left mine, his hands firm on my hips, guiding me exactly where he wanted me. As if I'd go anywhere else.

160

"You're so fucking beautiful," he murmured, his voice low and rough, full of need. His lips hovered just above mine. "I can't believe you're mine."

I sucked in a breath at his choice of words but didn't have time to respond before his lips were once more on mine. The kiss was deep, desperate for more, and filled with everything we'd been holding back for far too long.

Our warm-up in the shower had been just that—a warm-up. I needed more from him. I needed all of him.

Mine.

The word, fresh off his own lips, sent a shot through me. But the last thing I wanted to do was think about what it might mean.

My breath hitched and my fingers tangled in his damp hair. Cool air from the ceiling fan washed over me, a sharp contrast from the heat of my body, but it did nothing to cool the fire flowing through my veins.

Reid groaned, his hands tightening on my hips as he backed me up until my legs hit the mattress. His hands were there to steady me before I fell. His mouth trailed slow, deliberate kisses down the curve of my neck. A gasp escaped me as he lowered me down, his weight settling over me, his gaze dark with something I wasn't quite ready to name. But I knew I wanted this—I wanted *him.*

Badly.

"Reid." His name was little more than a plea on my lips.

He sucked in a breath and stilled above me. "You drive me crazy, Avery. In all the best ways." His fingers traced a slow path down my side, sending shivers up my spine and straight between my legs.

"Good." I reached for him and pulled him down. "Because I don't want you to stop."

He growled as his mouth found mine. With his tongue twisting with mine, Reid used his thick thigh to push my legs apart. I pressed my hips up to meet him, his hard length notched to my core.

We hadn't discussed birth control. The idea that I'd need to talk about such a thing with my husband struck me as funny, but I swallowed back my laughter when he pulled away, the question in his eyes.

"I'm on the Pill," I whispered. "And I'm...there hasn't been..."

"There hasn't been anyone else for me either," he said. "Not for a long time. It's only you, Avery."

His words and the way he looked at me made something deep inside me clench.

It's not real. It's not real.

But it sure as hell felt real when Reid's hand found my cheek, he tilted my head, looked me straight in the eyes, and said, "Only you."

Too many emotions slammed through me, so I did the only thing I knew to do. I kissed him. Every feeling I couldn't name, every emotion I was scared to acknowledge —I poured it all into that kiss.

I was completely lost to him. It was only when he thrust deep inside me that I once more found myself in the moment as I cried out.

Reid pulled away just enough to look at me. There was a storm of emotions in his eyes. I had to close my eyes to keep myself from getting pulled in.

"Avery. You..."

"Yes."

None of it made sense. It didn't have to. Because the only thing that *did* make sense was the moment. Him and me. Together.

"Yes," I said again as he moved rhythmically inside me, stoking the flames that burned brighter and brighter until finally, I couldn't hold it in for a moment longer.

My hands clawed at his back as my muscles tightened. A second later, my orgasm tore through me.

I cried out as my body rode wave after wave. I barely registered it as Reid took his own release, joining me in a powerful climax that left us both wrung out, exhausted, and, at the same time, completely and totally satisfied.

A moment later, he rolled to the side and pulled me with him so my head rested on his chest. I drifted off as he stroked my hair. The last thing I remembered thinking was how not only had he succeeded in taking my mind off my rough day, but he'd somehow managed to make me feel whole in a way I hadn't felt in a very long time.

Chapter Twenty-Six

Reid

FOR A MOMENT, I thought I might still be dreaming when I woke up to the morning light filtering through the curtains with Avery curled up against me, her hair fanned out over my chest and her small hand resting directly over my heart.

The memory of the night before hit like a slow, rolling wave. The way she'd looked at me like she saw something more than the gruff man everyone else assumed I was. The way she fit against me when she finally let go.

The only thing better was waking up with her in my arms.

Something had shifted between us the night before, and it was so much more than sex. Although, that had been a very welcome development in our relationship. Very welcome indeed.

My arm was slung around her waist, her bare skin soft beneath my rough palm. When was the last time I'd felt this...settled? Hell, had I ever?

Without wanting to wake her, I moved my hand so I could stroke her soft skin. She stirred in my arms, but her eyes remained closed, giving me a few more minutes of holding her.

Would she feel the same way when she woke up? As if there was more to this—to us—than just an arrangement? *And what if she didn't?*

I couldn't think about it. It wasn't an option. For better or worse, Avery was mine.

We'd shared vows.

Shitty vows, but vows nonetheless.

She shifted under my touch. A moment later, her eyes fluttered open. I waited while she woke fully, her eyes finally focusing on me.

"Morning." Her voice was husky, still full of sleep.

"Good morning."

I pressed my lips to hers gently and kissed her until she moaned against my mouth.

"Um." Avery touched her finger to her lips. "It certainly is."

Under the covers, her hands found my chest and slid lower down my body until she found the evidence of the arousal I'd woken up with. "Oh yes," she said. "It certainly is a good morning, isn't it?"

I sucked in a breath when she wrapped her hand around me and squeezed. As much as I'd love nothing more than to entertain exactly how *good* the morning could be, I'd already heard noises in the kitchen, and the reminder that Avery's cousin was still in our inn.

Our inn.

"It is a very good morning, sweetheart." My hand found

hers, and reluctantly, I moved it. "And as much as I'd love for you to make it even better…"

"Jacob?" she groaned.

"Jacob," I agreed. "I'll admit, I forgot about him last night. Then again, I was distracted."

In the very best way.

The trace of a smile crossed her lips, and I hoped she was remembering just how enjoyable our little distraction had been. After a moment, the smile faded and Avery rolled onto her back.

I shifted to my side and propped myself up on one elbow to watch her. Her eyes were closed, as if she could will her cousin away just by pretending he didn't exist.

She was quiet for so long, that I wondered whether she'd fallen asleep again. But finally, she exhaled a big breath and her eyes opened again. "Okay," she said. "I suppose he's not just going to go away, is he?"

"I'm not sure we're that lucky." I reached for her and brushed a stray lock of hair from her cheek.

She turned to me and gave me such a tender look, I wished in that moment I could take all the stress and worry away from her. I'd do anything to make this better for her.

Anything.

Including going to the stupid Sprout n' Shout and showing off our relationship in front of the entire town if that's what it took for Jacob to get the point—accept that we were not only together, we were *married* and he didn't have a hope in hell in succeeding in his efforts to take the inn away from us.

Us.

It was getting too easy to forget that it wasn't *ours*. The inn was Avery's. Our marriage wasn't real. When all this was over—*no.*

Not today. Not now.

I wasn't going to let myself think about what was going to happen when all this was over. Not after the night we shared. Even if it was temporary. Even if it was just for another day or two, she was mine.

And I was going to let myself enjoy every minute of it.

Chapter Twenty-Seven

Avery

FORTUNATELY, Jacob had already left for the day by the time I finally pulled myself away from Reid, stretched out my aching muscles, and made it out to the kitchen. Of course, he hadn't left a note—not that I'd expected him to—but no doubt he'd headed back to town to see whether he could dig up any more dirt on Reid and me and how our relationship wasn't real.

Wasn't it?

It sure felt real last night. It felt *very, very* real. And then again this morning when I'd woken in his arms. *That* had felt more real than anything I'd felt in a very long time. Safe, cared for, protected...*loved.*

It was ridiculous, certainly because there was no way there was any love between me and Reid this soon. Marriage or not. Yet...with him, I'd felt something I didn't remember ever feeling with Porter. Maybe it was just the gift of time and distance that had dulled my memories, but I didn't think so.

Reid was different. Being with him felt different.

"One sugar, no cream." I turned from the toaster as Reid handed me a cup of coffee.

"Yeah," I said dumbly. "You know how I take my coffee?" I blinked at him as he laughed.

"Of course I do." He leaned over and kissed my cheek. "You're my wife."

A full-body shiver rolled through my body. After a moment, I said, "Yes. I am."

Reid grinned. For a moment, my entire world spun, and I couldn't help but feel that even though it wasn't supposed to be anything more than a temporary arrangement between strangers, this was proof that it was more. It was so much more.

"At least for now," he said with a chuckle and reached past me as the toaster popped.

I'm glad he wasn't looking at me because I knew my face would have registered the hurt of his words. The truth they held.

At least for now.

I needed to remember that, or saying goodbye when the time came was going to be a whole hell of a lot harder.

"Right." I forced a cheerfulness I didn't feel into my voice. "What's the plan today? Do you need to go back to your shop or get any supplies from Grayson?"

I winced as I asked the question, knowing I was up to my eyeballs in debt with Grayson. He'd been kind enough to extend me credit. More than once. But I didn't know just how far his generosity would go, and small businesses had bills to pay, too. I didn't want to take advantage of him.

Especially when I didn't know when—or if—the money was ever going to come through.

I shook my head and took a sip of the hot coffee. I couldn't let myself think that way. The money *would* come through. I refused to believe any other option.

I literally couldn't afford to.

"What's with the serious look?" Reid was watching me, concern crinkling his handsome expression.

Without even realizing it, I'd gotten used to seeing the smile on his normally grumpy face. I'd grown used to the light dancing in his eyes. I didn't want it to be dimmed because of me.

"Everything okay, Avery?"

"Of course," I lied quickly. I took another sip of coffee, using the caffeine to fortify me. "After last night, and waking up to the perfect cup of coffee, what could possibly be wrong?"

I did my best to keep my voice flirty and light. It must have worked because, after a moment, Reid's lips twisted up into a cheeky grin. He reached for me, his arm snaking around my waist so he could pull me in close. "I couldn't agree more," he said, his voice rough and laced with desire. "I can only think of one thing that would have made this morning even better, and I blame myself for letting the opportunity slip through my fingers."

He kissed me, and I let myself sink into it. This might only be a temporary situation, but I'd be dammed if I wasn't going to make the most of every single minute.

"There's always tomorrow," I said with a wink when he finally pulled away.

He reached for me again, this time backing me up against the counter. "Forget tomorrow." The scruff on his chin scraped against my cheek. "I'm looking forward to tonight."

Somehow, after a few more minutes of making out like teenagers, Reid and I mustered up the willpower to pull ourselves apart and get to work. The list of things to do to get the inn ready was only growing longer by the day, and we had our sights set on the beginning of September to host the grand opening to the public and hopefully welcome our first guests.

The timeline was tight, particularly given the fact that I still didn't hold the necessary paperwork. But that was out of my control—at least for now. The only thing that was actually still in my control was getting the work done. Which meant, less making out and more actual work.

After Reid told me about the upcoming Sprout n' Shout, we decided to focus our attention on the gardens I'd been working on the day before and headed outside where the sun was already high in the sky.

Summer days in the mountains could be deceptive. It cooled down at night, but the days could get quite warm. And based on the heat early on, it looked like we were in for a hot one.

"You did a lot of work out here yesterday." Reid put his hands on his hips and assessed the yard, which looked kind of like either a backhoe or a dog with a bone had been let loose. There was dirt scattered all over the grass, and wilted piles of weeds that hadn't made it to the compost yet spotted the lawn.

"It's a mess." I shook my head, suddenly feeling overwhelmed with the task.

"Hey." Reid handed me a shovel. "It's nothing we can't handle. Let's start over there." He pointed to the far garden bed by the edge of the porch. "We can clear out the rest of those scraggly shrubs and get the ground ready for something fresh." Slowly, he turned his attention to the neglected flower beds along the path. "Over there would be a nice spot for some irises and peonies. You like those, don't you?" He winked at me before pointing to a different area of the garden. "And look at all the daisies hiding in there. If we clean out the weeds a bit more, we'll be able to see them. And who knows, maybe I'll pick you some bouquets like when we were kids. That would be—what?"

He stopped when he noticed me staring at him.

I couldn't help but chuckle and shake my head at the confusion lining his face.

"Seriously," Reid said. "Why are you looking at me like that?"

"The peonies. And…the daisies."

His face screwed up in confusion. "You don't like the idea?"

"I love it," I said, newly overwhelmed in a completely different way.

"Good." He leaned in and gave me a quick kiss on the cheek before once more turning to the garden. "In the fall, we can plant tulips and daffodils that will come up as soon as the snow melts and—you're staring at me again."

I couldn't help but laugh a little. "You're so cute when you talk about gardening."

"Cute?"

I nodded. "Cute."

"No one has ever described me as cute before."

"Well, I guess no one has ever noticed how cute you are when you have a shovel in your hand and you're talking plants." I stuck my tongue out and laughed at the dumb-struck expression on his face before it turned into a shriek when he dropped the shovel and started to chase me.

"I'll show you how cute I can be."

I wasn't sure whether it was a threat or a promise. Either way, I sprinted toward the wheelbarrow, putting it between us.

"You think I'm cute, do you?"

I laughed and dodged to the side, circling around the wheelbarrow. "I sure do."

"Then why are you running, Avery? Afraid I'll be too *cute* if I catch you?"

My core clenched with the promise held in his words.

Oh no, I'd be more than happy to let him catch me. Especially with the way his nostrils flared when he looked at me, desire in his eyes. Hell yes, Reid could catch me anytime.

But the chase was going to be fun, too.

"You assume that you *can* catch me." I grabbed the discarded gloves I'd left in the wheelbarrow and tossed them in his face before spinning on my heel and taking off across the lawn.

I'd only made it halfway to the path when I felt Reid's strong arms wrap around my waist.

I shrieked again as he lifted me off the ground and flipped me over his shoulder.

"Gotcha, sweetheart."

His palm clamped down on my denim shorts and squeezed. I groaned and wiggled against him, grinding into him.

"These shorts have been driving me crazy for weeks." His voice was rough with desire. "I'm going to enjoy getting you out of them."

So much for getting any work done.

But instead of walking me up the porch steps and back inside the house, a moment later, Reid flipped me over and, in a move so fast that it took my breath away, he had me flat on my back in the grass.

He loomed over me, caging me in with his arms. A shudder of desire rippled through me as he raked his hungry gaze over me. "Oh yes." His work-roughened hands slid greedily up my legs, stilling on my bare thighs. His thumbs moved back and forth on the sensitive skin there, dipping in and out of the hem of my shorts, moving closer and closer to my most sensitive spot between my legs that was already throbbing with need for him. "It's definitely time to get you out of these."

Reid's hands moved to the waist of my tiny shorts. He'd already managed to slip the button free before I remembered myself and the fact that we were currently on the front lawn of the inn where anyone and everyone in town could see us.

"Not here," I protested—albeit, not very hard. "Reid. We're—"

"I don't care." His pupils were blown.

"But, people will see."

"I don't care." He bent and kissed me until I also no longer cared.

It wasn't until he pulled away, tugging my lower lip gently between his teeth as he moved, that I came to my senses.

It was true I was completely gone for this man and how he made me feel. But I wasn't so far gone that all common sense had left my head. At least, not totally.

With my free hand, I reached out until it landed on what I was looking for. Before Reid realized what I was doing, I grabbed the nozzle, pointed and pulled the trigger, dousing my husband with a stream of ice-cold water from the hose.

Chapter Twenty-Eight

Reid

"IT'S GOING TO BE FUN." Avery squeezed my hand and led me down the sidewalk toward the community gardens and fields where the Sprout n' Shout was being held, just past the high school.

"Are you trying to convince yourself or me?"

"You, silly." She spun around and gave me a flash of her gorgeous smile.

I didn't know whether it was all the time she'd been spending outside lately, or maybe it was all the exercise we were getting inside at night, but whatever it was, Avery looked stunning.

I didn't think it was possible, but with every day that passed, she was more beautiful. Her skin was tanned, her cheeks just slightly pinked—or maybe that was the flush from the orgasms I'd given her right before leaving the house. She wore her long hair up in a loose twist, fastened with a clip I'd happily discard later so I could see the way her hair fell in curtains when she straddled my lap.

Taken with how amazing she looked, I stopped walking. Avery didn't. She reached the end of our arms and jerked, but before she could stumble, I pulled her back into my embrace with a quick spin.

Her mouth opened in surprise, but I kissed it away and cupped her cheek.

"What was that for?"

"I just wanted to tell you how pretty you look."

She laughed and shook her head. "You already told me that."

"Then let me tell you again." I kissed her lightly. "You are the most beautiful woman I've ever seen, Avery Ly— Walker." I spoke quickly to cover up the slip, but she'd noticed. Her lips dipped slightly before her smile recovered. "Walker," I said again. "Of course."

She hesitated for a moment, before she said, "A name change wasn't part of the deal, Mr. Lyons."

She had no idea how being reminded that what we were doing wasn't real had begun to sting.

Unaware of the dagger in my heart, Avery turned to continue walking, but I couldn't let it go one more minute without telling her something. Anything about how I was feeling. Talking about feelings or emotions was not some-thing I had any experience with at all, but neither was a fake marriage and that had been working out okay.

More than okay.

It had been working out really damn well.

The last few days with Avery had been amazing. And it wasn't just the sex, although that had been off-the-charts amazing. Together, we were fire and I couldn't get enough, evidenced by the fact that I'd almost lost control and taken her right on the front lawn of the inn a few days earlier. I would have, too, if she hadn't cooled me off when she had.

That was the thing. With Avery, I forgot about the world around me. Hell, I forgot about everything except for her. Because there was nothing else that mattered *besides* her. And with every minute that passed, it was a feeling that only grew stronger.

Before she could get away, I took a step and reached for her hand, tugging her back toward me one more time. Her eyes were wide with question as she spun to face me.

"Avery. I need to tell you something."

Instantly, her face shifted to worry. "Is everything okay?"

"It's fine." I cupped her cheek with one hand while the other rested on the swell of her hip. "No, it's better than fine. It's amazing. That's what I wanted to talk to you about, actually. These last few—"

"Hey, lovebirds!"

A slap on my back jarred me out of the moment. I spun to kick the ass of the jerk who dared to interrupt me before I told Avery how I felt about her.

"What the—Preston."

My youngest brother stood on the sidewalk behind us with a shit-eating grin on his face. "Did I interrupt something?"

I filled my lungs with a deep breath, using the time to calm down. It wouldn't do any good to punch my brother in the face in the middle of the street. No matter how much he deserved it for ruining what could have been a monumental moment between us.

"Yes."

"No."

Avery and I spoke at the same time.

She shot me a look before turning to Preston and holding out a hand to him. "Not at all. We were just heading to the Sprout n' Shout. Are you coming?"

There was no way Preston would be going to a plant festival. If it didn't involve snowboards in the winter or mountain bikes in the summer, my youngest brother didn't have the time of day for it.

"I'm sure he's—"

"Wouldn't miss it." Preston flashed me a cheeky grin.

Yes, I was definitely going to need to remind him who the older brother was.

"Great," Avery said. "Join us." She held both her arms out, inviting each of us to take one, which we did, and together, as an awkward threesome, we made our way toward the throngs of people who'd gathered at the end of the street.

Chapter Twenty-Nine

Avery

I HAD no expectations as to what a Sprout n' Shout would entail, but after just over an hour of visiting the many tables of various plants for sale or trade, I couldn't help but be impressed. The town of Trickle Creek was not only full of prolific gardeners, but everyone seemed to be in the mood to celebrate.

Besides plants, seedlings, and cuttings, there was an entire selection of artisans selling and showcasing their various handicrafts, a row of food trucks along the back of the field, and a smattering of musicians walking through the crowd, entertaining people.

I couldn't help but get caught up in the festive atmosphere around me. Somewhere around the table full of irises, Reid had begged off and gone in search of the beer gardens and his brothers.

Even though he wasn't right next to me, I could feel his presence. From time to time, when I turned around, I spotted him watching me. When he caught me looking, he'd wave, and more than once, I got a smile out of him. But only for a second before one of his brothers would elbow him in the ribs and no doubt give him a hard time.

As it turned out, my grumpy handyman wasn't nearly as grumpy as he'd have most people believe. At least not for me. I loved the way the warmth spread through me at the thought that Reid was *mine* and his sexy smiles were for me only.

"Well, if that isn't the look of a woman in love, I don't know what is."

Heat rushed to my face. I spun to see Lauren Westfield next to me. I didn't know her well, but we'd been introduced at the wedding and like most people in Trickle Creek, she'd been welcoming and warm.

"Sorry." Lauren laughed. "I didn't mean to embarrass you. I just think it's cute."

"Cute?" I forced myself to look away from Reid and focus on Lauren. "Really?"

"Oh my goodness." Lauren put her hand on my arm and squeezed. "It's been a long time since I've seen two people more over the moon for each other than the two of you."

Heat bloomed in my chest. *Love?* Was it?

I hadn't been in love with anyone since Porter, and it hadn't felt anything like what I was feeling for Reid. But I *was* feeling something for him.

I couldn't deny that.

This time with him had been refreshing and fun in a way I didn't even know I needed. Being with him had made the stress of the will and the inheritance so much easier. To the point where I was almost glad of the husband clause my grandparents had put in the will.

No, I *was* glad of it. I couldn't imagine doing any of this without Reid.

Aware I hadn't responded to Lauren, I smiled. "It's been a whirlwind," I said honestly. "But I wouldn't trade it for anything. Reid is just…" I sighed on my exhale, causing Lauren to laugh all over again.

"Oh yeah. You two are totally gone for each other. I haven't seen Reid look at a woman like that since…well, *ever.*"

"Really?" Besides the one time I mentioned my ex, and the fact that I'd once thought we'd get married, somehow Reid and I hadn't discussed our romantic history. It didn't really feel right considering we weren't actually a couple.

At least, we weren't.

But I'd be lying if I said I wasn't curious, and with the opportunity to learn a little more about him right in front of me, I couldn't help myself. "What were Reid's ex-girlfriends like?" I asked casually. "I mean, from another *woman's* perspective."

Lauren nodded as if she totally understood. "Well, I'd like to tell you something, but…"

"Oh, was his ex a friend of yours?" That made sense. It was a small town, where everyone knew everyone else. "Sorry, I shouldn't have asked."

"No." Lauren put her hand on my arm. "It's not that it's weird or anything. It's just that…well, Reid hasn't had a girlfriend."

My head snapped around. "What? Like, ever?"

"I mean, not since I've known him." Lauren shrugged

casually. "But from what little Brody's said, there was a girl-friend in high school who did him dirty and after that, he'd kind of sworn off women."

"Really?" That little bit of information made me sad for Reid. "That feels…"

"Lonely?" She nodded. "I think so." Her smile brightened again. "But now he's got you, so it all worked out the way it was supposed to."

A flash of guilt hit me in the chest. He *did* have me. But for how long? If Reid had gone almost his entire life without a relationship, it wasn't likely to change now. Especially not for someone he barely knew and was only doing a favor for.

No matter how I felt about him, and how I was quickly *starting* to feel for him, I needed to remind myself that it didn't mean he felt the same way.

It wasn't real.

I needed to remember that and *keep* remembering that. Or I was going to get hurt.

"Right," I managed to say when I realized Lauren was waiting for my response. "Now he has me."

"And we all think you're great."

Her smile was so warm as she looped her arm in mine, I had to ignore the feeling deep in my gut and hope she still felt the same when all this ended in Reid and I splitting up.

Thankfully, Lauren changed the subject a second later. "Hey, have you seen the lilacs that Geneva has at her table?"

"Lilacs?"

"For the inn." Lauren looked at me as if I'd missed the point of the entire festival.

Which, maybe I had because my mind was not on plants.

"Right. The inn."

Lauren laughed and looped her arm through mine. "Okay, okay. I know you're love-struck. But you do still have a grand opening to get ready for, don't you?"

"I do."

"Then let me help you," she said. "I love plants and gardening. I'm sure Reid's handy with a shovel, but you'll need a woman's touch when it comes to figuring out what to plant."

I didn't bother telling her about Reid's plans for daisies and peonies and how cute he looked when he was playing gardener.

Lauren's energy was infectious, and I enjoyed being around her. It wouldn't hurt to get another perspective and make a friend in the process. Happily, I let her lead me around the tables again and distract me from the confusion that continued to build in my heart.

Chapter Thirty

Reid

THE SPROUT N' Shout was only just getting started, with a full evening of activities planned, but I'd already had enough. All I really wanted to do was take my wife back to the privacy of our inn, take her to bed, and tell her that I was falling in love with her.

For real.

The only problem was that Avery looked like she was having a great time. The last few days had been stressful, to say the least. With Jacob hovering around and constantly poking at her about the inheritance, never mind the near-constant calls she'd been making to her lawyers, trying to figure everything out, Avery needed the opportunity to relax.

And it looked as if that was exactly what was happening. Together, she and Lauren were moving from table to table, their arms full of various plants that I knew I'd be planting in the next few days.

The smile on her face lit her up. She was gorgeous. Even more so when she laughed. I wished I could bring that kind of lightness to her all the time. I'd do anything for her.

Especially if it meant making her happy.

I leaned against one of the tall wooden tables my brothers and I had commandeered in the corner of the beer gardens, the designated drinking area of the festival, my beer in hand, only half listening to Ethan discussing the finer points of the drink and why his own brew would be so much better.

"I don't know," I said after a moment, tired of discussing the nuances of beer and why one was better than the other. "As long as it's cold, I'm happy." I lifted my plastic cup to my lips and drained half of it.

"You don't know what you're talking about." Ethan rolled his eyes. "Wait until you taste the brew I'm working on right now. It'll change your life."

"If a beer can change my life, I guess I'll be impressed."

"Reid doesn't need his life changed," Brody interrupted. "From where I stand, it looks pretty damn good to me. A brand-new wood shop, a big job to work on, *and* a pretty wife? Looks like you're winning at life, brother."

Internally I winced, but I couldn't let my brothers see. I hated lying to them. Even if it didn't *feel* like a lie anymore, it still was. But hopefully not for long.

"How *is* married life treating you, Reid?" Grayson asked, a glimmer of mischief in his eyes.

I still didn't know exactly what my twin thought he knew, and it wasn't the right time or place to get into it. But what I did know was that he needed to keep his mouth shut. At least for a little bit longer.

I'd clear it all up with him. Soon. In the meantime…I shot him a glare. "We're not talking about it."

"What aren't we talking about?" Preston joined us, a fresh round of drinks in his hands.

"Reid isn't talking about married life," Ethan supplied.

"He doesn't have to." Preston set the cups down on the table. "From what I hear, it's pretty damn wild."

My head snapped around. "Excuse me?"

My youngest brother laughed and held his hands up. "Simmer down, big guy. I'm only repeating what I've heard."

"Ohh, this sounds good." Brody leaned forward. "What have you heard?"

I elbowed him in the ribs—hard. "Who's talking about us?" I demanded.

"Everyone," Preston said to me before turning to Brody. "Turns out things got a little hot and heavy the other day on the front lawn of the inn."

Fuck.

"In broad daylight, too," Preston continued. "Looks like our boy here can't keep his hands off his new bride. I heard it was quite the show."

My face heated, my fists clenched, and I'd already taken a step toward him before Grayson stopped me.

"No," he said simply. "You are not doing this in the middle of the festival."

I turned to face my twin, ready to take him out to get to our baby brother if necessary.

"It's not his fault," Grayson said calmly. "Everyone's talking about it. I heard it, too."

"What?"

Ethan nodded, but Brody shrugged. "It was new to me," he said. "But damn, brother. Avery's a hottie and all, but the front lawn?"

"Shut your fucking mouth." I slipped from Grayson's grasp and was inches away from Brody before two more sets of hands were on me.

Brody just laughed as Preston and Ethan wrestled me back. "Enough," Ethan said. "What exactly is your problem today?"

I had a lot of problems. Mainly the piece of shit weasel currently living under our roof, making Avery's life hell. But there was also the intense conflict I felt about that asshole. Because as long as he was in Trickle Creek, it meant that I got to stay married to Avery and spend every waking moment making sure that everyone knew how *real* our union was.

And I'd be a lying bastard if I said I wasn't enjoying that part. Hell, I was a bastard either way.

"Nothing." I shook myself free from their grasp.

"Right. That's why you look like you want to punch something."

"Or someone," Preston added.

"Whatever." I turned around and backhanded a cup of beer off the table.

"Damn, Reid." Ethan glared at me. "I know it's shitty beer, but no beer deserves that."

"Honestly, I would have thought that a wife might have softened you a little bit," Brody added. "But you're still the same grumpy asshole you've ever been."

I shot him a look and bit back a growl.

"Oh no," Preston chimed in. "Our grumpy asshole

brother is a big softie for his wife. I've seen it with my own two eyes."

"Sounds like the entire town has seen it," Ethan added with a laugh.

I'd had enough of these assholes and this stupid plant festival, and I was more than ready to get out of there. With a grunt, I pushed away from the table, ready to take my leave.

Grayson caught up with me before I could slip away. "Hey." He grabbed my arm, and I spun around. My twin took a step back, both hands up. "Whoa. Your problem is not with me, man."

He wasn't wrong. I lowered my raised arm and mumbled an apology.

"This particularly sour mood wouldn't have anything to do with Avery's cousin, who's been lurking around town, prying into things, would it?"

I blew out a breath. It was a conversation I couldn't avoid much longer. And it was about a lot more than Avery's asshole cousin. "What do you know?"

He opened and shut his mouth, and then, to my surprise, Grayson shook his head. "I know you're both crazy for each other." He shrugged before crossing his arms over his chest. "She makes you smile in a way I've never seen you smile before. Not even when…well, not ever. And that's all I need to know, Reid." He paused, rubbing his chin and assessing me for a moment. "Unless, of course, you have something more you want to tell me?"

I did. Of course I did. Gray was my best friend. I told him everything. He was my sounding board for every important decision I'd ever made in my life. Keeping him in the dark on this had killed me.

I took a breath. "Gray," I started. "Avery and I—mother fucker." A flash of movement across the fairgrounds caught my attention. Instantly, all thoughts of confessing the truth to my brother were gone. There was only one thing that mattered.

Avery.

"What?" Grayson turned to see what I was looking at and saw it a second later. "Is that him?"

The look on my face must have given my brother the answer he needed because he put a hand on my arm to still me. "Don't make a scene, Reid. It's not worth it."

"I'm not going to make a scene. Why would you even say that?"

"Because you look like you're about to tear his head off, man. And trust me when I say that is *not* a good idea. Not in front of the entire town, and not in front of Avery. You don't want to do that, Reid. You know you don't."

Dammit.

I shook off his touch. "Fine." He had a point, even if I didn't want to admit it. I was a grumpy asshole. That wasn't a secret—Avery knew that. But what she didn't know was that I also had a temper when someone wronged someone I loved, and I didn't want her to find out. And hell, that was mostly because I never wanted to see her wronged.

Because I loved her.

The realization slammed into me, causing me to take a step backward.

Fuck. Me.

I loved Avery. I loved my *wife*.

Yes, I knew I was developing feelings for her. But love? I wasn't sure how to process that.

And standing in the middle of the Sprout n' Shout, surrounded by everyone I knew, wasn't the time or place to attempt to figure it out. Especially when Jacob had spotted my gorgeous wife and was cutting through the crowd, headed directly over to her.

I couldn't see the look on his face or what he was saying to her. But I didn't need to because Avery's body language said everything I needed to know.

Chapter Thirty-One

Avery

"THIS ONE NEEDS FULL SUN." Lauren thrust a potted plant of some kind into my hands. I'd lost track of all the different types she'd already pointed out, but I was pretty sure we'd already seen one just like this. "It'll be great next to the porch," she continued. "Maybe three or four of them alternating in colors would be nice. Speaking of colors, have you thought about a color palette yet?"

"A color palette for the garden?"

"I know, I know." She laughed and took the plant from my hands. "We should have discussed that before we started shopping, but I got carried away."

"That's okay." I turned, dumbfounded, toward the wagon Lauren had borrowed about ten minutes earlier. It was loaded with all kinds of smaller plants and flowers. The bigger shrubs and even a few trees that she'd picked out were being held behind the tables. Lauren suggested we send Reid and his brothers to pick them up later, and I couldn't argue with that. As it was, I was starting to think we should abandon all our selections for them to haul back to the inn later. Especially considering I was starting to hit my limit with gardening.

"You know what?" Lauren led me by the arm away from the table. "You look like you might need to get out of the sun."

"Is it that obvious?"

My new friend laughed. "I tend to get excited about gardening," she said. "And I know not everyone is as passionate about plants as I am. I'm sorry. I can be a bit much sometimes."

"No." I stopped her. "You're just the right amount. Honestly. I'm just…" I scanned the crowd, suddenly missing Reid's solid presence at my side. It caught me off guard how much I'd grown used to having him close by. We'd spent so much time together over the last few weeks. It was funny because we hadn't even been separated very long, but I missed him.

The ridiculousness of it struck me as funny, and I threw my head back in a deep laugh.

"Oh yeah." Lauren grabbed my hand. "We need to get you out of the sun for a bit. Come on, we'll get you a drink."

Happily, I let her start to lead me through the crowd. But we'd only made it a few steps before a familiar voice sent chills down my spine.

"I know what you're up to."

The voice cut through the air like the snap of a brittle branch.

I stopped so suddenly, Lauren jerked against my hand and almost fell over before she broke away.

"Avery." Jacob's voice was different. The way he spoke my name was different than before. It was demanding and colder than usual.

I took a breath, letting it fill my lungs before exhaling. It was only then that I turned slowly, my pulse thudding against my ribs. He stood close. Too close. His smile was practiced and forced, but it was the look in his eyes that stilled me.

"Jacob." I assessed him. "Nice that you could make it to the Sprout n' Shout. These town events are—"

"Cut the crap, Avery. I know what you're up to."

Anger curled through me. This man had made my life hell for too long, and judging by the look on his face, he was poised to do even more damage. This time in front of the entire town. Still, I wouldn't give him the satisfaction of knowing he'd gotten to me.

"I'm shopping for plants." I waved in Lauren's direction. "Lauren has been using her expertise to help me pick out some new plants for the inn and replace the—"

"I know you're lying, Avery."

Ice ran down my spine. "What are you talking about?"

"You know exactly what I'm talking about." He took a step toward me. His lips were twisted up into a sick version of a smile. His eyes flashed with hatred.

I never did understand where his anger toward me came from. It couldn't be only because Grandma and Grandpa left me the inn. This had started years earlier.

"You and your *husband*." His words were full of disdain.

"You're lying. And you've been lying from the beginning. And I can prove it."

Finally, I broke out of my trance. I needed to defuse him quickly. Everyone in town was watching. I couldn't afford to let anyone hear his crazy theories.

Theories that held far too much truth to be safe.

I held out my hand. "Why don't we go talk somewhere?"

"I don't think so." Ignoring my hand, he shook his head and glared at me. "We can talk right here. Or are you hiding something from all these nice people?" Jacob waved his arms around to encompass the crowd that had at some point formed a circle around us.

There was no getting away from this. My heart raced and I couldn't feel my toes, but somehow I stood my ground.

"I'm not hiding anything."

"Bullshit!"

"Jacob. I don't know what you think you know, but I—"

"I know you and Reid aren't really married."

Someone in the crowd gasped, but I didn't take my eyes off Jacob.

"That's not true," I said calmly. "Judge Baker married us himself and—"

"Whatever." He practically spat the word at me. "It might be *legal*," he used his fingers to make air quotes, "but that doesn't mean it's *real*."

"You're not making any sense, Jacob." I hoped my voice sounded calm and patient despite the panic that was very quickly bubbling up inside me.

"Enough." He took another step toward me as he raised

his voice. "I'm not stupid, Avery. And, quite frankly, the fact that you think I'm as gullible as all these people is insulting."

Another gasp, along with a few grunts of protest at being called gullible sounded around me. But it didn't deter Jacob.

"I don't know why they gave it to you," he said with distaste. "But no doubt you conned our grandparents into thinking that you were their favorite somewhere along the line. The only saving grace is that they were just old school enough to make sure you couldn't have it on your own." His eyes flared.

I needed to stop him, but I couldn't make words come out of my mouth. I stood frozen like a deer in headlights, watching the wreckage barreling toward me.

"You needed a husband to get the inn." He delivered the truth like a bomb. "So you found one, didn't you? The first one who agreed, I assume."

I shook my head slowly. My pulse pounded in my ears. "No. I mean, yes. But not like—"

"I have to admit, cousin," Jacob's smirk deepened, and his voice dripped with condescension, "I didn't think you had it in you to take all this on. The inn, the renovation, and now a fake husband. You surprise me, Avery. But what I still can't figure out is what you had to do to convince him to marry you."

I thought I was going to be sick. I swayed on my feet, but there was nothing to grab onto. I knew Lauren was behind me somewhere, but I didn't dare take my eyes off Jacob during his assault on my life.

"It's not—"

"What did you have to promise him, Avery? Or did you just have to open your—"

A blur of movement rushed past me.

And then a sickening crack.

Jacob's head snapped back, his body jolting with the force of the punch. He staggered a moment, his eyes wide before he crumpled to the ground in a heap of stunned silence.

Shock startled me from my stupor. My hand flew to my mouth, and I spun to see my husband. He stood over Jacob, fists still clenched, his chest rising and falling with barely controlled fury. His jaw was tight, his eyes dark and burning with something lethal.

I didn't recognize him.

"Reid." His name was barely more than a whisper from my mouth. His lips twitched a little, but he didn't turn away from Jacob.

"Reid," I said again, and put my hand lightly on his arm.

My touch seemed to break him from his focus on my cousin. He turned and looked at me; his face softened immediately.

"Avery, I—"

"What the fuck, man?"

Reid spun on his heel and once more loomed over Jacob. "That was for the way you were speaking to my *wife*," he growled. "Don't try to get up or I'll give you a reason to stay down."

I threaded my arm through Reid's and pulled him back before he could make good on his threat. "Everyone is watching," I hissed in his ear. I needed to get him out of there before things got worse. Not that they could possibly get any worse than they already were. But I didn't want to stick around and find out.

"Let them watch," Reid muttered. "Everyone should know that they can't fuck with you, Avery. I won't let them mess with my wife."

I didn't like this caveman version of him, but despite that, I couldn't help but feel a flicker of heat deep in my belly at his protectiveness. "Let's go, Reid." I tugged him. "Please."

It must have been the plea in my voice that finally made him move. To my great relief, he let me start leading him through the crowd, that parted to let us through.

"This isn't over," Jacob called out behind us. "You'll hear from my lawyer."

I had no doubt we would.

Only this time, I didn't know whether it would be in regard to the inn, or to press assault charges against Reid.

I couldn't decide which was worse.

Chapter Thirty-Two

Reid

MY KNUCKLES THROBBED, but I barely felt the pain with the fire still burning in my veins. That asshole was lucky the whole town was watching. He deserved far worse for the way he was talking to Avery.

My breath came hard and fast as Avery dragged me out of the festival grounds, away from the crowd. She moved fast, her grip tight on my wrist as if I might try to turn around and finish what I started.

Hell, maybe I would have. I should have hit him harder and made sure the bastard stayed down. Only now, Avery was looking at *me* like I was the problem, and that just twisted the anger in my gut tighter.

She stopped moving abruptly once we were far enough away. "Reid, what the hell was that?" She spun on me, her eyes blazing. "You can't just go around punching people."

"The hell I can't. And I'd do it again. He deserved it."

"He did not." She put her hands on her hips, and a flare

of completely inappropriate desire shot through me. "No one deserves to be punched."

"They sure as fuck do when they're talking to you that way." My pulse throbbed in my head. I needed to calm down, but I was way too wound up. "Nobody can talk to my wife that way."

"I'm not your wife."

"The fuck you aren't."

She took a staggering step back. I reached for her and pulled her back, but she shook my arm off. "You know this isn't real, Reid. This wasn't supposed to be anything more than..."

"Don't say that." I wasn't going to stand by and let her dismiss everything between us. Not so carelessly, and not when I knew she didn't mean it. There was no way she could mean it. But I also knew it wasn't the time or place to get into this. Not with so many people who could overhear us. If she wanted to blow us up, that was one thing. But I wasn't going to let her throw it all away. Not when she was so close to the inn being hers for good. "Not here." I glanced around. "Don't—"

"It's over." She shook her head and looked down. "He already knows, Reid."

"Jacob doesn't know shit." Again, I moved to reach for her, needing to feel her, but something in her gaze stopped me. "Avery?"

She looked so defeated. So sad that it broke my heart.

"He doesn't." I softened my voice and tried again. "Nothing is over. It doesn't have to be. Not unless..." I couldn't bring myself to say it.

She turned away, and the anger that had only barely

died down burned hot and fast again. Jacob did this. He'd taken a strong, carefree, optimistic woman full of hope for the future and turned her into a sad shell of who she'd been when she'd first arrived in Trickle Creek.

I'd fucking kill him.

As if Avery could read my mind, she turned again. "Don't," was all she said.

I forced my hands to relax at my side. "Don't what?"

She blew out a breath but didn't answer me right away.

"Avery?"

"Don't make it worse, Reid. Worse than you already have."

"Worse?" I turned and paced across the sidewalk and back. "Worse? You think *I* made it worse? Seriously, Avery? How could I possibly make this fucked-up situation any worse than it already was?"

I hated myself for raising my voice at her. She didn't deserve it. She didn't deserve any of this. But I was so frustrated I didn't know what else to do.

"He's going to press charges, Reid. How is it made any *better* if you go to jail?"

Fuck. I didn't think of that.

"I'm not going to go to jail. I was defending you."

"There were witnesses." She dropped her face in her hands. "And he *is* the type to press charges, Reid. This isn't going away. None of this."

I could see it on her face. She was giving up.

"He's going to press charges and use that as leverage to prove that our marriage isn't real. He's going to get the inn, Reid. He's going to get it, and I'm—"

"No." I gathered her up in my arms and held her tight

to my chest. It wasn't going to end this way. I *refused* to let it end this way. I refused to let it end at all. "Avery. It will be okay. I promise. I will take care of it. I will take care of everything. You're not going to lose the inn." I stroked her hair, inhaling her sweet scent while I murmured what I hoped were reassuring words in her ear.

But she didn't soften in my embrace the way I expected her to. She didn't wrap her arms around me and sink into my touch. Instead, she held herself stiff until I took a step back.

"I need to be alone, Reid."

Her words stabbed me in the chest. "Avery, I don't—"

"I think you should maybe stay somewhere else tonight."

"What? No. I'm not—"

"It's too complicated," she said. "And with Jacob at the inn, having you there will be—"

"You're not seriously going to let that son of a bitch set one foot back inside our inn, are you?"

"It's *my* inn, Reid." Her expression hardened. "At least for the moment."

I took a step toward her, but she held a hand out to stop me. "Go, Reid. Please. You've already made this worse than it needed to be. I just…" She dropped her head.

And while I stood by and watched, Avery turned and walked away from me, leaving me standing alone on the sidewalk with nothing to do but watch her go.

Chapter Thirty-Three

Avery

JACOB WASN'T there when I got back to the inn. Truthfully, I wasn't sure he'd have the balls to come back after everything that had happened, but I knew him well enough to know that he liked a fight.

Especially when he had the upper hand.

And in this instance, he did.

And he knew it.

Not physically, of course. Reid definitely had it over him in that regard. But Jacob wasn't an idiot. He'd use Reid's momentary loss of control to his advantage.

I dropped my head into my hands. Everything was such a mess. Worse than before, if that was even possible.

I could almost hear my mom's words in my ears.

After my grandfather's funeral, when the will was read and I learned about my inheritance, she hadn't seemed surprised. All she'd said was, "I'd hoped they'd changed their mind. That inn is going to be the same anchor on you as it was on them."

But I didn't see it that way. *At least, I hadn't.*

I saw the laughter and the love. I saw mornings at the kitchen table with piles of Grandma's waffles. The way Grandpa would tell her they were the best waffles he'd ever had, even if he'd had one just like it the day before. And then how Grandma would blush a little, and wave off the compliment before turning around with a big smile on her face.

The inn was always a bustle of activity, and every day was different. People were coming and going, and each of them had a story that my grandparents were more than happy to sit and listen to. They had a kind word for everyone, and every single person who stayed under this roof left feeling better for it.

When I pictured the inn and their life here, I saw the way they'd sit on the porch swing every night, Grandma curled up under his arm while they talked about the day and their guests. I saw the love. I *felt* it.

I wanted it. I wanted that life.

I wanted the inn.

And now…

It looked like I was going to lose everything: the life, the love, *and* the inn.

To my surprise, it wasn't the prospect of losing the inn that hurt my heart the most.

I poured myself a glass of wine and retreated to the porch for some fresh air.

I choked back a sob when I saw the empty chairs still

dangling from the porch roof where my beloved swing once hung. We still hadn't gotten around to fixing it and now—

My phone rang. The sharp sound sliced through the quiet evening as my heart leapt into my throat.

I'd told him to leave me alone, but now that I was alone, I wanted nothing more than for Reid to be there with me. I snatched up the phone without looking at the screen and accepted the call. "Reid, I—"

"Hello to you, too, Avery."

"Mom." My heart fell, which wasn't fair. Despite our differences, I loved my mom. "I was just thinking about you."

"All good things, I'm sure." She laughed, and despite my exhaustion, the sound warmed me. "How are you, dear? I haven't heard from you in ages."

I know it wasn't intended, but guilt flared through me. I'd purposely kept my mom in the dark about the drama surrounding my inheritance. I didn't want to give her any reason to worry, but if I was being honest, I really didn't want her opinion on the whole situation. Never mind the fact that I'd gotten married and not told her. That was a whole different issue.

I knew what she'd say. And right now, it didn't feel like there was enough room in my heart for the truth.

"I'm doing great." I tried for light and fun. "It's been really busy around here getting everything ready for the grand opening, and today there was a thing called the Sprout n' Shout. It was—"

"Avery." The tone of my mom's voice told me she could see directly through my bullshit. "What's really going on?"

I wasn't ready to concede defeat. "What makes you think there's anything—"

"Avery." She waited a beat. "I heard you got married."

"Oh."

"Yes," she said. "Oh."

I exhaled slowly and pinched the bridge of my nose. There was no point lying to her. At least not any more than I already had. Especially considering she was there for the will reading. She knew what it said. And she knew very well I wasn't in any position to get married before that moment.

"It turned out that the lawyers weren't able to dismiss that particular part of the will."

"So you figured out a way around it."

It wasn't a question but I nodded anyway, even though she couldn't see me.

"Oh, Avery." Her voice didn't hold any judgment. Only sadness and worry. "Put me on video."

I did as she requested, pushing the button that changed our call to a video. Seeing my mom's face on the screen had the immediate effect of bringing tears to my eyes. Or maybe it was everything else that had happened, coupled with my complete and total exhaustion. Either way, seeing the way my mom was looking at me with so much worry and concern broke me, and the tears spilled down my cheeks.

"Sweetheart." Her voice was full of love. "What's going on? What happened?"

"You were right," I said after a moment. "This was a bad idea. The inn…Trickle Creek…all of it. It was a horrible idea. I've maxed out every credit card I have, and borrowed against my savings." I ignored the shock on her face at my confession and kept going. There was so much more. "I paid the handyman I barely knew to marry me so I wouldn't lose it all, and then Jacob showed up, threatening to take it all away from me. And he did. Or at least he's going to. He figured it out and he made a big scene at the festival and then Reid punched him and I got mad and yelled and sent him away and now my heart is breaking because somehow, somewhere along the way, I fell in love with him but we can never be together, because our entire relationship is a lie and—"

"Wait."

My breath hitched and another sob tore from deep inside me. I was a mess. Tears poured freely down my face, streaking my cheeks with the mascara I hardly ever wore.

"I just wish he was here with me, but I don't know where he is and I—"

"Avery," she said gently. "Stop."

I did.

"Take a breath, honey."

I did as I was told.

"Now," she said. "There's a lot to unpack there. So, let's start with the most important part."

I nodded.

"This man? You love him?"

My heart squeezed in my chest, and I nodded, reality settling in. "I do, Mom. I've never loved anyone the way I love him."

"I can see that, honey." Her smile was kind. "But have you told him that?"

Chapter Thirty-Four

Reid

I RAN the chisel down the edge of the board, shaving the thin curl of wood off the already perfect board until it fell to the workbench below, joining the growing pile of shavings and scraps.

I should be paying attention to the cut and the feel of the grain of wood under my hand, but all I could think about was Avery.

And the look on her face when she told me to go.

She was angry with me. And she had every right to be.

I'd let my temper get the best of me. It had been years since I'd lost control like that. There was a time in my life when it was a regular occurrence that I got into a fight with someone.

A short fuse, my mom called it.

I'd always had one. When we were kids, we fought like most brothers did, especially when my brothers would play a game with one another to see how far they could push me until I exploded. By the time we got to high school, I didn't need any help getting heated enough to throw a punch.

But instead of my brothers, it was generally some other dickhead who'd pissed me off or flirted with my girl. Grayson and Brody spent more time than they should have pulling me off some asshole. She'd never come right out and said it was my temper that had driven her away, but Isabella did tell me before she left that the guy she'd cheated on me with was *calmer* and less *explosive*.

It was the reality check I needed. I'd done the work. I'd learned to channel my temper into more productive pastimes than fist fighting. I'd learned to love woodworking, and I'd gotten damn good at it, too.

I was still a grumpy asshole—that wasn't a secret. But I was no longer a grumpy asshole who'd throw a punch.

Until today.

"Dammit." I slammed my palms down flat on the board, shaking the sawdust off the top, and dropped my head. No wonder Avery didn't want me around. I'd fucked up.

Badly.

Emotion roiled in my gut, but the rage from earlier was gone. Now, it was replaced by something I wasn't completely sure of. A mixture of regret and hurt and…*love*.

Abandoning the chisel, I reached for a piece of sand-paper instead. But before I could get back to work, the sound of the door sliding open pulled my attention. I didn't have to turn around to know who'd joined me.

"Thought you might be here."

"Figured you might come looking for me." I lifted my head to see my twin brother watching me, his arms crossed over his chest. "You didn't think I'd be at the inn?"

Grayson shook his head. "Not tonight. Not after…"

"After I just epically fucked things up, you mean?"

He only shrugged. "Are you ready to talk to me, brother?"

There didn't seem to be any reason not to. Not anymore.

"Come on," Gray said. "I'm sure you have a beer in here somewhere."

He wasn't wrong. I led him through the shop to the back wall where the little fridge was stocked with some growler jugs of Ethan's early test samples of his microbrew.

I poured us each a glass. It wasn't until I'd had my first sip that I took a deep breath and repeated the question I'd asked him once before. "What do you know?"

Grayson took a minute to answer, as if he were weighing the options of how much he should say.

Finally, I said, "I'm not going to lose my shit."

"I'm not worried that you'll punch me, Reid." He looked me dead in the eyes. "I'm worried that you'll screw up what is very likely the best thing that's ever happened to you because you're too stubborn to see what's right in front of you."

I opened my mouth to protest, but he held up his hand to stop me.

"No. Let me say this, brother. And hear what I have to say."

I sucked in a breath but held my tongue.

He leaned back against the workbench and crossed his arms as if he were settling in for a long overdue conversation. Maybe he was.

"I know you better than anyone," he started. "And I've

seen you go through a lot, man. I've seen you pissed, hurt-
ing, and generally angry at the world. Hell, I've even seen
you pretend you don't care when we both know you do. But
I've never seen you like this."

I gritted my teeth, no longer sure I wanted to hear what
he had to say. "Like what?"

Grayson took another sip of his beer, wiped the back of
his mouth, and gave me a look that only a twin brother who
knew me better than I knew myself could give. "Like you're
falling hard and fast and scared as hell to admit it to yourself because then you're going to have to do something
about it instead of hiding away in your bloody workshop
with your head so full of sawdust you don't have to face the
truth."

The words hit harder than I expected. I exhaled through
my nose and dropped my gaze to the floor while I absorbed
what he said.

My hands found the edge of the workbench, needing
something solid to hold onto.

"I see the way you are with her," Grayson continued.
"She means something to you. Something a whole lot more
than whatever deal you made."

My head shot up, and I stared at him, open-mouthed.

"Yes," Gray said with a knowing grin. "I know your
marriage started with some kind of arrangement between
the two of you. I'm sure it had something to do with the inn,
and maybe this wood shop. But I don't need to know the
details. They don't matter. The only thing that matters is
that whatever has happened between the two of you since
you took your vows, it's a whole lot more than what brought
you together in the first place. I see the way you look at her,

Reid. And I see the way she looks right back. There's nothing fake about any of it. Not for a second."

I stayed quiet, because what could I say? He wasn't wrong.

Grayson sighed and ran a hand over his chin. "You're in love with her." He spoke the words simply. "*That* is what I know. And that is the only thing that matters."

His words settled over me. I *was* in love. But coming to that realization with such clarity no longer mattered because it didn't make it any easier to fix what I'd already broken.

When I didn't speak right away, Grayson shook his head and reached for his beer again. "I get it, Reid. You're scared to let yourself want something real or let yourself care about someone that way. But if you don't tell her how you feel, you're going to regret it for the rest of your life. And I'd hate to have to be the one to say *I told you so*."

"Yeah." I let out a dry laugh and shook my head. "I bet you'd hate that."

Grayson smirked. "I sure would." He pushed up against the workbench and clapped me on my shoulder. "Seriously, no pressure, Reid. But don't screw this up, okay? She's a damn good woman. And more importantly, she's good for you."

Didn't I know it.

"She hates me, Gray." I shook my head and kicked at a chunk of scrap wood. "I fucked it all up. I never should have punched that douchebag and now—"

"No." He stopped me. "You totally should have punched him. I've never seen a bigger piece of shit deserve to be knocked out more than that guy."

I stared at my peacemaker brother.

"I'm serious," he said. "But maybe you shouldn't have done it with a couple hundred witnesses is all."

I laughed. "Isn't that the truth?" It only took a second for reality to hit me again and for the laughter to die on my lips. "That piece of shit is trying to take Avery's inn from her. I'm afraid I just made it all worse. She'll never forgive me."

"Sure she will. Maybe you should start with an apology."

He sounded so confident, I almost believed him.

"I don't know." I shook my head. "You didn't see her face, Gray." I huffed out a breath and walked away from the back bench and my brother. I headed straight toward the project I'd been working on. Now, more than ever, I needed to finish it.

A moment later, my twin was behind me. "What are you working on?"

I ran a hand over the well-sanded wood and took a deep breath. "My apology."

Chapter Thirty-Five

Avery

I WOKE up with a dull throb behind my eyes. The kind that came from too little sleep and too much thinking. It had been a long night of tossing and turning. The bed felt empty without Reid. It was cold without his arms around me.

Or maybe it was just the ache in my heart from his absence.

My mind had spun all night with the mess I'd made. I'd turned it over a million ways in my mind, but for the life of me, I couldn't figure out a way to sort it. The truth about our marriage was out. Or, it would be as soon as Jacob opened his mouth and found someone who'd listen to him.

And they would. Because he wasn't wrong, and as soon as people learned about the clause in the will, they'd see our quickie marriage for what it really was.

Everything was slipping through my fingers. It was a reality I'd finally accepted sometime before dawn.

I was going to lose the inn. And all my savings. I'd be bankrupt with the debts I owed.

But that wasn't the reason my chest felt tight.

Reid.

I never really had him, and I'd already lost him.

Never mind the fact that I wouldn't be able to pay him the rest of the money we'd agreed on and that he needed for his wood shop. I'd kept the financial details from him as much as possible, but I owed it to him to tell him the truth and give him a heads-up. It wasn't a conversation I was looking forward to.

With a sigh, I dragged myself out of bed. Lying there wasn't going to change anything. As much as I would have liked to hide from reality a little bit longer—or forever—I knew it wasn't going to hide from me.

Stepping outside, I took a minute on the porch to take in the lawn and the half-dug-up gardens, waiting for all the plants we'd picked out the day before. I wondered what had happened to them. *Had Lauren taken them, or were they still down at the festival grounds?*

It didn't matter anymore.

I turned slowly, unable to look at the upturned dirt any longer without crying. That's when I saw it.

The swing.

It hung from two new chains exactly where the old one had been.

Reid.

I walked toward it slowly, still not quite believing what I was looking at. My fingers brushed over the smooth wood. It was beautiful and obviously made with so much attention to detail.

The edges were rounded, every inch of it carefully sanded until the wood was almost soft. The seat was wide, with plenty of space to curl up with a book and cup of tea. Or a lover.

The craftsmanship was unmistakable—Reid had made this. Not just thrown together, but made with care and precision.

For me.

I swallowed back the lump in my throat.

A breeze stirred the swing a little, swaying it back and forth. Something inside me moved along with it.

This was real.

It wasn't an act. Or part of our deal.

He'd built me something beautiful. Something strong. Something that would last.

And I had no idea what to do with that.

So I did the only thing I could think of.

I sat.

And I cried.

For my grandparents and what they'd built together and the love they'd shared. The same love they gave to me and impressed upon me for all those summers I spent right here with them.

I cried because I missed them more than I'd let myself even think about. Being at the inn had been a way of having them back. Even for a little bit, in the smallest way.

It hadn't been much, and there was still so much to do, but every day when I grabbed a paintbrush or a hammer and set to work putting things right and bringing life back into the old building and the *home* that had brought so much joy to so many, I felt like I was bringing *them* back.

It was stupid, sure, but…it also wasn't.

Saying goodbye to the inn was saying goodbye to them.

Tears streamed down my face as I tucked my legs up under me and gently swayed back and forth.

I gave in to the tears and let myself grieve properly for the first time since I'd said goodbye to my grandfather.

I don't know how long I sat there, but it was long enough for my tears to dry on my cheeks and for the emptiness in my chest to bloom into a dull, unrelenting ache.

It wasn't just the loss of the inn I was grieving, and I could be honest enough with myself to admit it. It was Trickle Creek, too.

The community.

The people.

The new friends who very quickly were feeling like old friends.

It was Reid.

It was *so* much Reid.

I let my hand slip from my lap and rest on the hard wood beside me. He'd built this for me.

Even after we fought. Even after I told him to go and that I wanted him to leave me alone. Even after I'd given him every reason not to, he'd still done this.

For me.

That meant something. It had to.

I hugged my legs close to my chest. I let my other hand drape over the back of the swing, and that's when I felt it.

There was something carved in the wood.

I couldn't see it from my angle, so I unwound myself, stood, and walked around the swing.

"Oh." My hand moved to cover my mouth as fresh tears slipped from my eyes. "Reid."

My fingers traced over the carving he'd made in the back of the swing.

A mountain range in the background, with two larch trees side by side in the foreground.

Just like the trees my grandparents had planted.

A sign of resilience, strength, and *change.*

Resilience.

Strength.

Change.

I traced my fingers over and over the carving until finally, I knew what to do.

Chapter Thirty-Six

Reid

MAYBE SHE WASN'T COMING.

Maybe I'd gotten it wrong.

It was possible I'd misread the entire situation and she was angrier than I thought. Or worse, she didn't feel the same way I did.

But that wasn't it. It couldn't be.

I knew in my heart she'd come. And that counted for something.

I'd started work on the swing weeks earlier but it wasn't until I was halfway through construction when I got the idea for the carving. It was right after the night when she'd shown me the trees her grandparents had planted. It also happened to be when I first realized that even though I didn't know yet what they were, I had real feelings for the bubbly blonde who'd burst into my life and asked me to marry her.

Thankfully, Grayson had agreed to help me with a middle-of-the-night mission to hang it. We'd managed not to wake any neighbors or have the cops called on us with our fervent whispers and more than one curse word hurled at each other in the dark.

But that wasn't the hard part.

The hard part was waiting.

I hadn't gotten more than five minutes of sleep all night. I'd tossed and turned, consumed by questions and second-guessing. *Had it been enough? Would she understand the swing was more than a peace offering? Would she understand how I felt?*

And if she did, would she feel the same?

I'd cleaned every inch of my shop, stacked and organized every piece of wood at least twice, and even gone through the scrap box to find any salvageable piece. She still hadn't called.

It had been hours. Surely she would have seen the swing by now. She would know it was me...she would... "Screw it."

There was no way I was waiting another minute for her to come to me. I needed to go find her. I grabbed my truck keys and was almost out the door when it flew open.

"Uncle Reid!"

My niece stood in the doorway, her face flushed, her hair slipping from her ponytail, and her eyes wild.

"Quinn? What's wrong?" Everything else forgotten, I rushed to her, grabbed her by the forearms, and began to assess her for damage. "Are you okay? Where does it—"

"I'm fine." She shook me off. "Why didn't you answer your phone? Everyone's been calling you."

"My..." I turned and patted the back pockets of my jeans. "I don't have...shit. I must have lost it at the—"

"It doesn't matter." Quinn grabbed my hand. "You have to come with me. Hurry."

"What? Where?" I let her lead me from the shop, pausing only long enough to slip the padlock into place. "What's going on, Quinn?"

"It's Avery." She tugged the passenger door of the truck open and stood on the running board, looking over the truck at me. "Judge Baker called an emergency meeting," she said. "He's making a ruling on the will."

"What?" I was frozen in place. "Now?"

"Yes." She slapped her hand on the roof of the truck. "*Now!* You need to hurry, Uncle Reid. Let's *go!*"

I shook my head and jumped into my truck, jamming the keys into the ignition. "Fuck." The word slipped out before I realized my audience. "Shit," I said. "Sorry. Dammit." I shook my head. "Don't tell your dad I said any of that."

Quinn laughed. "Right." Her voice dripped with sarcasm. "Because I've never heard it before."

I couldn't help but grin despite the worry rushing through me. If the judge called an emergency meeting, what did that mean? Was it because of Jacob? Of course it was because of Jacob and the stunt he'd pulled at the festival. Damn him. I would *not* let that asshole be the reason Avery lost the inn. It wasn't happening.

My foot fell hard on the accelerator, urging the old truck to move faster.

Chapter Thirty-Seven

Avery

BLACK CLOUDS THREATENED OVERHEAD. The weather had turned quickly, but it seemed fitting and matched my mood perfectly.

I'd only been awake a few hours, but it had been a rollercoaster already. The moment of hope, when I saw the carving on the swing, seemed like it happened a million years ago.

Before I could go to Reid, my phone rang with a call from my lawyer, William, alerting me to an emergency meeting that Judge Baker had called regarding his final decision on the will. It seemed that he wasn't a fan of public spectacles in his town, and wanted the matter settled once and for all.

"Good morning, Avery." William appeared next to me, his briefcase in hand. He patted my arm and gave me a friendly smile. "Are you ready for this?"

I shrugged before making myself offer up a smile I

didn't feel. "I guess so. We knew it was coming sooner or later, right? It'll be nice to have it resolved."

William gave me a kind smile that didn't give away anything. I knew he'd tried his best for me. He'd argued my case and presented all the proof of our marriage. But ultimately, if the judge decided our union wasn't legitimate, there was nothing he could do. There was also a chance that the judge could press charges or hold me in contempt if he decided we'd lied and committed fraud.

I couldn't think about that possibility. Not yet. One thing at a time.

A cool breeze washed over me.

"Did you hear from Reid yet?"

I shook my head before pulling my phone from my purse again. Three unanswered calls and two unanswered texts. *Why wasn't he answering me?*

He couldn't be angry with me? It didn't make any sense. Not after the gift of the swing. I wouldn't let myself think anything bad. There had to be an easy explanation for where Reid was and why he was ignoring me.

I didn't have time to find him, so I'd called Grayson and he'd promised to take care of it. But the meeting was supposed to start right away and there still wasn't any word from him.

My gaze kept scanning the plaza for some sign of him. I expected him to pop around the corner at any moment, ready to stand by my side for the judgment. After all, he *was* my husband.

But he wasn't there.

And I needed him. More than I realized.

"Are you ready to do this?"

No. I wanted to scream. Instead, I sucked in a breath and as bravely as I could, nodded.

William waved me in the direction of the judge's private office, where my fate would be decided. But before I could move, I heard footsteps approaching from behind.

I turned and my stomach immediately clenched in a mixture of disappointment and disgust to see my cousin approach. I know it was wrong, but I took a measure of satisfaction to see the blue and purple bruise under his eye.

"You're late, Jacob."

"I didn't come here to play nice, Avery."

"Yeah." I crossed my arms over my chest. "I got that. Where's your lawyer? Or are you self-represented?" I knew he wasn't. He'd hired a shark of an attorney from the city.

"He'll join us remotely." He raised one eyebrow. "Where's your *husband?*"

I didn't miss the sneer in his voice. He made a show of looking up and down the plaza for Reid, who still hadn't appeared. I was beginning to think he wasn't going to. Maybe I'd read the entire situation wrong.

The ache in my chest was only dulled by the anxiety that crashed through every nerve in my body. I worked hard to keep my breathing level and my heart rate steady. I refused to let Jacob see how he'd gotten to me. I wouldn't give him that satisfaction.

When I didn't answer, Jacob chuckled. "Shocking." He rolled his eyes dramatically. "He disappeared as soon as the money dried up, huh?"

I hugged my arms around my waist to keep my hands from shaking.

"I guess I should give him some credit though," Jacob

continued. "He's smart enough to know when to quit. The jig's up, Avery. You should take a note from your partner in crime and hand it over. You lost. You've been exposed for the fraud that you are. And Reid's absence today proves—"

"It proves nothing, you jackass."

My heart leapt in my throat at the familiar voice. Before I could turn to confirm it with my own eyes, Reid's arm slipped around my waist and pulled me close. The heat from his body warmed me. Instinctively, I leaned in closer.

"Sorry I'm late," he whispered as he kissed me on the cheek. "I came as soon as I heard what was happening."

I looked up into his eyes, searching for the answers to every single unasked question I had. And I had many. But now wasn't the time. "Thank you for coming," I said instead. "I can't tell you what it—"

"Avery." Reid turned me and cupped my cheek. "I need you to—"

"Give it up already." Jacob stepped forward, his sharp voice slicing between us. "We all know the two of you are full of shit. You're just making fools of yourself now."

Reid sucked in a breath and squeezed his eyes shut. I could see the effort he was putting in to keep his anger in check.

"Why don't we just wait until we hear from Judge Baker." William stepped forward and put a hand on Jacob's shoulder but my cousin shook him off.

"We don't need to wait," he sneered. "We already know. This is fake." He waved toward Reid and me. "And I can prove it."

He couldn't. No one could. Not really.

"I have witnesses that can verify you hired Reid to do

the renovations on the inn, mere days before you got married."

"That doesn't *prove* anything, you asshat." Reid had turned to face Jacob head-on. He'd released his hold on me to stand with his arms crossed over his broad chest. He looked formidable. "Except that you are grasping at straws."

"I don't think I am, hotshot." Jacob's smug expression soured my stomach. "I have proof that the day after your *wedding* also happened to be the day that you put the down payment down on your fancy new wood shop. Which leads me, and anyone else with half a working brain, to believe that my pretty little cousin here *paid* you to be her husband so that she could meet the terms of our grandfather's will that *required* her to have a husband."

Somewhere, someone behind me let out a gasp. It was only then that I realized we'd once again managed to draw an audience to our family drama. An audience that was very quickly learning the truth of our deception. Even if Jacob didn't have any actual proof, I had to admit that hearing it from his lips, it all sounded pretty damming.

I took a step back, away from Reid. If I was going down —and it seemed that I was—I wasn't going to let him go down with me.

"Without that husband," Jacob continued his rant, "not only would the inn not go to Avery, but she'd also lose the cash inheritance that goes with it."

"That money is for fixing up the inn, Jacob. It's not for—"

"It doesn't matter, does it, cuz?" His voice dripped with poison.

When had he started hating me so much?

This wasn't what our grandparents would have wanted. Everything was such a mess.

I shook my head and instinctively looked for an escape route.

There wasn't one.

The crowd had only grown around us.

My stomach sank. I looked to William for guidance, but he was staring at his phone, typing quickly to someone on the other end.

I couldn't bring myself to look at Reid.

It was over.

I shook my head, focused on my cousin, and took a step toward him. "You're right, Jacob."

Chapter Thirty-Eight

Reid

WHAT THE FUCK was she doing?

Jacob was *not* right.

Well, maybe he was.

In *theory*.

But screw theory. It didn't matter.

Avery stepped away from me and toward her douchebag cousin. She was going to confess everything in front of the entire town, and I refused to let her throw away everything she—no, *we*—had worked so hard for.

She stood at the front of the crowd, her hands clenched at her side, her chin lifted in that stubborn way that left no room to guess what she was about to do.

The audience of shoppers and nosy townspeople were silent, hanging on every word, waiting for her to confirm everything Jacob had been saying all along—that our marriage was a lie. That she tricked them all.

And I was only an innocent bystander in this mess.

Like hell I was.

Before she could open her mouth and say the words that would destroy everything, I moved.

"No." My voice rang out, cutting through the gloomy mid-morning air, through the weight of her guilt and right through the distance between us.

"Reid." She turned and looked at me, her eyes imploring. "Don't—"

"No," I repeated, firmer this time, looking straight at her —not the crowd; not Judge Baker, who I thought I saw from the corner of my eye, pushing his way through the crowd for a better view; not Jacob, who was no doubt fuming and purple in the face.

It was just her. I only had eyes for Avery.

"You don't get to do this," I told her. "You don't get to take the fall for something that isn't a lie."

Her breath hitched; her shoulders rose and fell in despair. Her lips parted but I didn't give her the chance to speak. Because I needed to say this. I should have said it ages ago. Hell, I should've said it a long damn time ago.

"You want to tell them our marriage was fake?" I shook my head, stepping closer, eyes locked on hers. "Then explain to me why you're the first thing I think about when I wake up. Tell me why I catch myself looking for you whenever you're not near. Why every single time you smile at me, it feels like my world makes sense, even if it's only for a second."

A murmur rippled through the crowd, but I didn't hear them. I only saw her—Avery, the love of my life, standing there, looking at me like she couldn't decide whether to run away or throw herself into my arms.

Jacob stepped forward, trying to interrupt. "This is ridiculous. You've just admitted it was a fake marriage. You're in breach of the conditions of the will. You've—"

"Shut up, Jacob," I snapped in his direction. It only took one look from me for him to shrink back. "I'm busy right now, but I will shut you up myself if I have to."

A few people laughed, but I didn't care about that either.

I refocused on the only thing that mattered and took another step toward Avery, my voice dropping, softening. "You drive me crazy, Avery. In all the best possible ways. You're a menace with a shovel, and I'm not sure you'll make it as a painter."

Her lips twitched a little, but still, she didn't smile.

"But that's one of the best parts of you. You don't care if you're the best at it…you just want to do it. You will do everything and anything it takes to bring the inn back to life because you care so much that you can't imagine any other option."

I saw the way she sucked in a breath and her hand pressed flat on her chest.

"But what you don't see is that you've already brought it back to life," I continued. "Yes, it still needs some more paint, and the gardens are a mess right now and there's an endless list of things we still need to get to, but none of that matters. You've already achieved what you set out to do, no matter what happens, Avery. You did it. The moment you set foot in the Tamarack Inn again, or more specifically, the moment I shoved you through the window," I winked and finally, she smiled, "that was the moment that place came back to life."

A single tear slipped down her cheek. I wanted more than anything to go to her and wipe it away, but I needed to finish.

"You are all warmth and light and without a doubt the most beautiful person I've ever met. And you're pretty cute, too." I smiled at her because that's what she did. She brought it out in me. "You make me a better man, Avery. Just being in your presence makes me feel *good*. You walk into a room and people feel it. It's an energy that gives people hope. Like this world isn't as hard as it felt a second ago."

"Reid, I don't—"

"You do." I took her hand in both of mine and held it against my chest. "You see the best in people, even when they don't deserve it." I jerked my head to the side where I knew Jacob must be fuming. "You see possibilities where other people see nothing but rubble and ruins. And somewhere along the line, your sunshine slipped through the cracks of my grumpy crust and lit up something inside me that I didn't even know needed to see the light of day." I couldn't keep the smile off my face if I tried. My heart pounded, and I was sure she could feel it, but I didn't care. I wasn't trying to hide anything from her.

I was completely and totally lost to her. I was hers. In every way. I just hoped like hell she'd let herself be mine.

"I love you, Avery." My voice was rough but steady. "Not because of this mess we're in. Not because of the inn. Or because of anything else but the simple fact that I cannot imagine waking up in a world where you are not beside me. I love you because you are the sunshine and second chances and everything I never knew I needed in my life. And I will spend every single day of the rest of my life proving it to you, if you'll let me."

"Reid." Her voice hitched. Tears streamed down her face now, but I refused to let go of her hands.

"I don't want to just be the man who helps you rebuild the inn, Avery. I want so much more than that. Maybe it's selfish of me, but I don't care because I want to be the man who gets to build the life you want. The life you *deserve*. I want to be the man who gets to love you for the rest of our days."

"Reid…"

"Tell me you want the same thing. Tell me I'm not crazy and I didn't just make a fool of myself in front of half the town."

She exhaled sharply, and the smile I'd been missing for the last few days, finally, mercifully returned to her face, filling my heart with the love that'd been missing since she walked away from me outside of the Sprout n' Shout.

Avery didn't answer me. Instead, she pulled her hand free of mine, grabbed the front of my shirt, and pulled me down into a kiss that was anything but pretend.

The entire world fell away as I pulled her close, taking everything she was willing to give me.

The crowd erupted, cheers and gaps filling the air around us, but it barely registered over the pounding of my heart. Avery let out a breathless laugh, her hands still gripping my shirt like she was afraid to ever let go.

When she pulled back, her eyes were shining, but they were no longer filled with sadness. I vowed to never let that happen again. Not if I could help it.

"Reid?"

I dipped my head in a nod and waited.

"I love you, too."

The words melted the little bit of doubt still left in me. I cupped her face in my hands and used my thumbs to wipe the tears from her cheeks. "I can't tell you how happy that makes me, sweetheart."

"You don't have to. I can see it on your grumpy, handsome face." She laughed, dropping her head back. "This is not how I saw today going."

I laughed. "Me neither, to be fair. But I had full intentions of not letting you walk away from me again without making sure you knew exactly how I felt about you."

Her hand slipped to the back of my neck. She held me firm as she looked into my eyes. "Well, I know now."

"Good."

"You don't really think this is going to fix anything though, do you?"

"Unfortunately, no. But whatever it is that's going to happen next, I'm not going to let you face it alone."

She threw her arms around my neck and hugged me again.

I meant it. I didn't know what was going to happen. If it meant she lost the inn or I lost the wood shop, as long as we didn't lose each other, Avery was all I needed.

I closed my eyes and let myself savor this one moment with my girl before reality crashed back in. It wasn't long enough before a strong voice broke through.

"I can tell you what will happen next."

Chapter Thirty-Nine

Avery

I DIDN'T WANT to leave the comfort of Reid's arms. Not now that I knew he felt the same way I did. Not ever.

Belatedly, I remembered we were in the middle of the plaza, outside Judge Baker's private office. And not only were we now officially late for the meeting that was going to decide my fate in this town, but half of the townspeople stood by to bear witness.

We'd already provided enough entertainment, so why not give them a little more?

Reluctantly, I tore myself out of Reid's embrace but stayed close to his side. He wrapped his arm tight around my waist as we turned to face the judge who was watching us with a bemused expression.

"Sorry, Judge. I didn't mean to—"

"No apology necessary." He held up a hand to stop me. "I can tell you had a few things that needed to be discussed."

My cheeks flared with embarrassment and the realization that we'd just inadvertently exposed our deception.

"Finally." Jacob pushed his way toward us, coming to stand shoulder to shoulder with the judge, who gave him a sharp look until he took half a step to the side. "We're late to get started with the meeting. We should go—"

"I think we can do it right here," Judge Baker declared. "After all, it doesn't seem like there are any secrets left to spill, are there?" He looked at each of us in turn.

Reid and I both shook our heads.

Jacob pulled his phone from his pocket. "Let me get my lawyer on the line. I'll need him to—"

"He's right here."

We all turned to see my lawyer, William, holding his phone up. A man I didn't recognize was on the screen. "I called him a few minutes ago," William said. "I thought he might want to see and hear what was going on."

What the hell?

I shot William a look. *Did he really have Jacob's lawyer on a video chat? Whose side was he on?*

But I didn't have time to ask either of those questions, because the man in question spoke up from his small screen. "And I thank you very much for that, William. I wasn't aware of the exact nature of the relationship between Ms. Walker and Mr. Lyons. This has been most enlightening."

"See?" Jacob turned to the phone, speaking to his lawyer. "Now you understand what I've been trying to tell you. It's not real. None of this is real, which means that they're both liars and—"

"Enough." It was Judge Baker who spoke up. There was no room for argument in his voice.

Above us, the clouds had darkened and at some point, while we'd been standing there, the wind had picked up. A storm was coming.

"They admitted it, Judge." Jacob turned to the older man, who did not look impressed. "You heard it, too. It's not real."

"What I heard was the two of them declare their love for each other," he said pointedly. "What I *saw* was a very public display of that love. And what I *know* is that I married the two of them myself in my chambers and that is my signature on their marriage certificate."

My body started to shake. From the growing cold or the nerves, I couldn't be sure. The judge's voice gave nothing away.

Jacob opened his mouth to protest, but the judge cut him off with another sharp look.

"That being said, there is the matter of the will that needs to be discussed and settled once and for all." He looked at each of us in turn.

Reid nodded and had the sense to look chastised. I offered the judge a small apologetic smile. And of course, Jacob crossed his arms, looking smug. I forced myself not to look at him. I couldn't let myself be bothered by my cousin. Not anymore.

No matter what the judge said, it would be fine. I had Reid. I could handle anything with him by my side.

At least I hoped I could.

"I'm only going to go through this once," the judge began. "So I want you all to listen carefully because my decision is final."

We all nodded.

"The Walkers' will, that was both legal and binding, very clearly stated that Ms. Avery Walker and her *husband* were to inherit the inn along with the funds that have been set aside and invested for the purposes of renovating and running the inn."

I'd heard it before. Multiple times. I nodded and dropped my gaze to the ground.

"Now, given the very specific nature of the conditions, the precise wording, and the fact that the original document was drafted many years ago in a different time for society, I'm apt to agree with Ms. Walker and her counsel that the requirement of the spouse be dismissed."

Hope soared within me.

"However," the judge continued. "That is not what is going to happen in this case."

I didn't miss the self-satisfied sound that slipped from Jacob. I swallowed hard against my feelings and waited for the verdict.

"What is going to happen is that Ms. Walker and her *husband*, Mr. Reid Lyons, will be rightfully and completely awarded full possession and ownership of the Tamarack Inn, along with the entirety of the funds that have been set aside as stated in the Walkers' original will and testament. Effective immediately."

"What?" Jacob yelled. "That's bullshit. This is fake," he said. "Didn't you hear them? They just admitted it in front of the entire town. The marriage is fake. They've been playing all of you. They deserve to be in jail, not rewarded with—"

"That is enough, Mr. Walker. I told you my decision was final."

Reid squeezed my shoulder, shaking me a little.

It was only then that I dared look up. "Did he just say what I think he said?"

Reid's smile told me everything I needed to know.

"But…I thought…"

"No." Jacob's rage-fueled voice cut through the air. "I refuse to accept this." He snatched the phone from William's hand and spoke to his lawyer. "We'll fight this. We'll expose their lie and—"

"No, Jacob." His lawyer, from his office on the other end of the phone, was calm and controlled. "I don't know if you were listening earlier, but I was. This case was lost before it began. What I witnessed was two people very much in love with each other and very much in a legal marriage. Even through the phone, I could see that. There is no case here."

"What?" Jacob's face turned an awkward shade of purple. "You're fired." He shoved the phone back at William and spun on his heel, looking for a way out of the crowd that had begun to close in, ready to congratulate us on officially owning the inn.

"This isn't over, Avery," he spat in my direction.

"Oh yes, it is, Jacob." Reid's arm held me close as he pulled me slightly behind him and stepped up to Jacob. "This is very much over. And I suggest, for your own sake, you get out of town."

"Are you threatening me?"

"No." To my surprise, Reid chuckled and shook his head. "I'm not. You're not worth my time, but I think there are a few others who might have a different opinion." He raised his eyebrows and jerked his head toward the crowd that now included all of Reid's brothers, who'd joined at some point when I wasn't paying attention.

"Avery," Jacob tried again. "We can talk about this."

Reid tried again to steer me away, but I needed to face him. "No," I said as I turned to face him. "We can *not* talk about this, Jacob. You heard the judge. The inn is mine—" I stopped myself and reached for Reid's hand. "It's *ours*." I gave him a smile, and he squeezed my hand in return before I continued. "It's just as Grandma and Grandpa wanted," I told my cousin. "You can either accept that or not. That's up to you. But either way, we're done here."

I exhaled and released the tension I'd been holding, right as the clouds finally opened up and the rain started.

Reid

Avery shrieked as the rain started, but it quickly turned into a laugh as I tugged on her hand and started running, leading her through the crowd.

We moved through the throngs of our friends and neighbors, all of whom cheered us on and offered us congratulations until we were finally free and I got her under the shelter of the gazebo that had been placed in the center of the plaza to honor the late Michael Carlson, the savior of town.

Surprisingly, the gazebo was empty. What was left of the crowd was still gathered at the far end on the plaza, while everyone else had scattered into the coffee shop and other stores, seeking shelter or going about their business now that the show was over.

And it was over. Finally.

I spun my wife in my arms and held her close.

Her hair was wet and pasted in strands to her face. Her dress clung to her in all the right places, and she'd never looked more beautiful.

"Damn, I'm a lucky man." I pulled her close and kissed her hard. "For so many reasons, but mostly because I had the good fortune to be in the hardware store that day when you walked into my life."

"I'm just lucky you agreed to help me break in." She laughed and it was the sweetest sound.

Now that her smile had returned to her face, I never wanted it to leave. I would do everything in my power to make sure it never did.

Overhead, the rain pounded on the roof, the warm smell of cedar filling the air around us.

"Can you believe it?" She shook her head. "Can you believe it's over?"

"Sweetheart, it's nowhere near over." I reached out and brushed a wet strand from her cheek. I pulled her close again because I needed to feel her—*my wife*—against me. Exactly where she belonged. "It's only just beginning."

Chapter Forty

Avery

I WASN'T sure what woke me first: the golden light slipping through the curtains, or the solid weight of Reid pressed against me. I sighed, stretching a little.

But as soon as I moved, a voice, thick with sleep, murmured, "Don't."

I turned to see Reid, his eyes still closed, his hand splayed over my stomach, keeping me exactly where he wanted me.

"Don't what?"

"Don't get out of this bed." His eyes opened, meeting mine.

"I have things to do," I teased but made no attempt to leave.

"Yes," he said seriously. "You do. Right here." He tugged me closer. "With me."

He trailed a finger down my belly to the top of my thigh; I shivered with the need he stirred in me so effortlessly. "Everything else can wait." He lifted himself so he loomed over me as his fingers moved lower until they were between my thighs.

I groaned and let my legs fall open in invitation. "Maybe they can wait a bit longer."

"No maybe about it, sweetheart." He kissed me deeply while his fingers worked their magic. Moments later, the only thing on my to-do list was coming, long and hard.

Which was exactly what I did.

And then again a few minutes later, when my sexy husband made love to me. It was slow and easy and absolutely the perfect way to start the day after the stress of the last few days.

"I could get used to this," I murmured against his chest when I was finally able to formulate coherent thoughts again.

"That's a good thing because you're not going to be able to get rid of me now."

I liked the sound of that. Very much.

I must have drifted off again, content in the afterglow of multiple satisfying orgasms, because the next thing I remembered was waking up to the rich aroma of coffee. When I opened my eyes, Reid was gone.

I felt a flash of disappointment, but only for a moment before I heard him in the kitchen, whistling. *He was still there. And this time, he wasn't going anywhere, because he loved me.*

The thought warmed me and put a huge smile on my face. A smile I was still wearing a few minutes later when I was dressed and joined him in the kitchen.

"Oh." He frowned in my direction. "I was going to bring you coffee in bed."

"Sorry." I kissed him on the cheek. "I appreciate the thought, but I had a different idea."

I took the mug he offered me and led him out to the porch and the swing he'd made for me.

"Ah." A little grin twitched over his lips.

I settled onto the seat and patted the space next to me. The swing was already amazing and beautiful, but sharing it with Reid, his arm around me, his body weight gently rocking it back and forth, was absolute perfection.

"So, you like it?" His voice was casual, but I didn't miss the weight behind the question, as if my answer truly mattered.

"Like it?" I ran my hand over the smooth wood and closed my eyes, remembering how it felt the first time I saw it.

Was that really only yesterday?

I swallowed past the rising emotion and reached across the space between us to take his hand. "No," I said softly as my fingers twined through his. "I love it, Reid. It's the most perfect gift I've ever received. You're so talented. I had no idea. Honestly."

His mouth twitched as if he were trying not to look too pleased with himself, and it made me laugh.

I twisted in the seat and tucked my legs up under me so I could face him. "No one has ever given me something like this before, let alone made me something so incredibly special. Thank you."

His gaze finally met mine. There was something unreadable in his dark eyes. "You don't have to thank me."

"Yes, I do." The gesture was more than just a gift, and we both knew it. It was about thought and feeling. It was about knowing exactly what I wanted—what I *needed*—without me even saying it.

His jaw shifted, as if he wasn't quite sure what to say next.

So I made it easy on him. "If I'd known you were secretly so romantic, I might have fallen for you a whole lot sooner."

That made him laugh. "Sooner than the first time you saw me in the hardware store?"

I smacked him lightly on the arm. "You're so cocky. Besides, I meant it when I said I started to fall for you when I saw you with Quinn for the first time."

"Because you saw how sweet I really was." He wiggled his eyebrows, and I shook my head. "You want to know the moment I knew you were going to be it for me?"

I did. I very much wanted to know.

He grinned at me. "It was that day in the Bean Bag when you told Danny Davis you'd already hired me and assumed I would say yes."

"I knew you would."

"How could I say no after that?"

"You couldn't. That was my plan." I giggled, but the laughter dissolved when I realized what he'd said. "But… that means…"

He nodded. "That was it for me, sweetheart. I knew then that you were going to change my life." Reid shrugged a little. "I just don't think I knew how you'd spin me so totally out of control."

I laughed again and snuggled close. "In all the best ways."

"You know it."

We sat like that for a few minutes, rocking gently together on our swing on the inn that was now officially and legally *ours*.

It wasn't just the swing that had been built to last. It was the Tamarack Inn. And most importantly, it was us.

Chapter Forty-One

Reid

THERE WAS no way around it. I knew it going in. Still, I didn't expect family dinner to be quite so obnoxious, with every member of my family alternating between offering me congratulations and cursing me out for lying to them.

I guess I deserved it.

Still.

Now that the truth was out and there were no more secrets about anything, you'd think they'd just let it go.

We were married.

Avery was part of the family.

She wasn't losing the inn.

Everything was good now.

They needed to get over it.

And they would.

But I knew my siblings and I knew that they loved any opportunity to give one another a hard time. I also knew that, as a general rule, we didn't lie to one another. And despite how many times my brothers told me they understood, I know it still stung that I'd deceived them—or tried to—in such a major way.

I was going to feel bad about that for a while. And that was mostly why every time I was the butt of one of their jokes at the family dinner, or they raised their glasses in yet another toast to the *happy couple*, I simply swallowed down my annoyance and smiled.

Besides, celebrating Avery and the fact that not only was she legally my wife, but she was *really* my wife, was never going to get old.

I looked at her now across the room, talking with my twin, and felt such a surge of love it took me by surprise.

"That's not a look I'm used to seeing on your face, brother." Ethan elbowed me sharply in the ribs as he sat down next to me. He handed me a glass of beer. "Try this one. It's a lager."

I took a sip. "I like this one." I wiped my lips with the back of my hand. "Way better than that hoppy shit."

"Hey. IPAs are very popular right now."

"Sure they are." I shook my head and took another drink of the crisp, cool liquid. "With the hipster, bougie crowd. But real men like real beer. I'm glad to see you're going to offer some drinkable brews."

Ethan laughed and smacked me on the back. "It's good to see that marriage hasn't softened all the grump right out of you," he said. "You wouldn't be the same old Reid if you weren't still a grumpy asshole."

I scowled at him and shook my head.

"Seriously, brother. I know we're giving you a hard time, but we're all really happy for you both. Avery's awesome."

"She sure is."

"Obviously we would have preferred it if you'd let us in on the secret, but I think I speak for all of us when I say that we understand. It was a complicated situation."

To say the least. No one was happier than I that it was over and done with.

The day after Judge Baker's final decision, Avery and I, along with her lawyer, William, had joined him in his office to sign off officially on the paperwork. Shortly after, I had William draw up the paperwork that would put the inn in Avery's name only.

I planned to spend the rest of my life with her running the Tamarack Inn, raising a family, and generally being happier than I ever had in my whole life.

But the inn was hers. It always had been and it always would be.

"How did Mom handle the news?" Ethan asked, and I groaned.

Calling our mother and telling her about my marriage to Avery for the first time had been difficult, but somehow she'd appreciated the romance of the story I'd spun for her that we just couldn't imagine waiting a moment longer and rushed into our vows.

When I told her the truth, she was less understanding and had given me a piece of her mind. Not that I expected any less. I knew that once she met Avery, all would be forgotten. She'd always wanted a daughter, and there was no doubt she'd fall in love with her daughter-in-law just as quickly as everyone else had.

"She'll be okay," I told him. "Or she won't." I shrugged. "I can't change things now." Nor would I want to. Although

I didn't love everything about the way it went down, I wouldn't change it because, at the end of it all, I got Avery. And that's all that mattered.

Ethan laughed and raised his glass to me. "Congrats, brother." We clinked glasses.

I'd just taken a drink of my beer when Quinn ran up behind me and wrapped her arms around my shoulders in an aggressive bear hug. "Uncle Reid! Did you hear the news?"

Somehow I managed to swallow my beer before reaching around me and grabbing my niece in an effort to unwind her from my back. I took a moment to give her an extra hug. I was lucky my niece was so easygoing.

I'd begged her for forgiveness and done my best to explain why the whole situation was necessary in a way that a twelve-year-old might understand. I needn't have worried, though. Quinn had only shrugged, told me she thought Avery was great and made me swear that she wouldn't interfere with our ice cream dates, and that was the end of it.

"What news?" I asked when I finally had her in front of me.

"Dad's opening an official brewery," she said excitedly. "It's going to have tables and chairs and everything like a proper bar but it's not a bar," she added quickly, looking at her dad. "Because Dad said I won't be able to go into a bar. But a brewery is different, so even though it will be full of beer, it's cool for me to hang out there."

I waited until my niece had stopped spewing words at me before looking at Ethan. "A brewery? Like a real one?"

He laughed. "Yup. Turns out that even with all your

woodworking crap out of there, the shed still isn't big enough. I decided to go for it and give it a shot. Why not?"

"Why not?" I grinned and raised my glass. "I'll cheers to that. Especially with this very drinkable, manly beer."

He laughed. "Thanks, brother. It's not as exciting as your news, but I'm pretty thrilled about it."

"I'd say. And it's *very* exciting. I can't believe you didn't say anything sooner."

Ethan shrugged.

It was Quinn who offered more details. "Dad said you had enough going on that we shouldn't bother you with—"

"It's not a bother."

"That's not how I meant it." Ethan shot his daughter a look.

I chuckled and shook my head. Quinn was the truth-teller in the family, for sure. She definitely kept us all on our toes. "Okay, fill me in."

Happily, Ethan spent the next few minutes filling me in, and I couldn't have been happier for my brother. It had been his dream for years to have his own business in Trickle Creek and a brewery was a perfect fit.

"Now that you have your own shop, I want you to make the bar tops for the brewery. I want to show off your talent."

"I'd really like that, brother." The warm glow of pride filled me. "Thank you. Really. It means a lot that you'd ask."

"Of course." He grinned. "I know you're busy with the inn, so you have some time. But not too much."

I got the sense I didn't have much time at all. "When are you opening exactly, Ethan?"

"Well…"

"Ethan."

My brother laughed, and once again, it was his daughter who gave him up. "Dad already got the space."

"Is that right? Where is it?"

"In the old Chinese food spot next to the bookstore at the west end of the plaza."

"Really?" I was genuinely surprised. "I actually don't think I've been in there." The property was often referred to as the old Chinese restaurant, but it had been vacant for almost ten years. "Next to the bookstore?"

"Isn't it great?" Quinn piped up. "I love that store. I could *live* there."

"Yeah." Ethan lowered his voice. "Except I don't actually think the owner feels the same way."

I gave my brother a look. "About Quinn living in her shop, or the fact that you're moving in next door?"

He raised his eyebrows, and I laughed.

"I'm sure that Delaney will be fine with it. I've met her a few times, and she seems like a reasonable person. And I get the impression she's pretty quiet, but I'm sure she'll be a good neighbor."

"Delaney's great!" Quinn offered. "She knows so much about books and she lets me read as many as I want."

"It's not a library," Ethan said with a shake of his head before focusing on me again. "I hope she'll be a good neighbor. Because there's no turning back. The equipment is supposed to come by the end of August."

"August?"

"Well, we won't open then. But I was aiming for Thanksgiving."

"Thanksgiving? As in Canadian Thanksgiving? In October?"

"Obviously Canadian Thanksgiving." Ethan shook his head with a chuckle. "Think you can handle that schedule?"

It would be tight if we wanted the inn to open for the Labor Day long weekend, but for my brother, I'd do it. "No problem."

"I knew I could count on you."

Avery's laughter on the other side of the backyard caught my attention. She looked so light and free, with her head thrown back in laughter at something Grayson and Preston said. She was always stunning, but in the last few days as the stress of the inn and the finances had cleared up, she had a whole new glow about her. I couldn't take my eyes off her.

I'd been apart from my wife for too long. "If you'll excuse me." I stood and made my excuses to Quinn and Ethan. "I think it's time I got my beautiful wife home."

"But it's so early! Why do they have to go so early?" I heard Quinn protest, and Ethan answered with a chuckle and a reassurance that she'd understand when she was older.

Chapter Forty-Two

Avery

"THAT WAS FUN." It was a perfect summer evening. The type of night where the heat of the day had given away to the perfect temperature, where it was still warm enough not to have a sweater, but cool enough that I looked forward to snuggling with Reid on our swing. It was very quickly becoming one of my favorite parts of the day. "Your family is so nice and really cool with everything."

"I don't know how cool they are about it." He shook his head. "But they do seem to love you, and I think that helps soften the blow of it all."

"It's more than that." I tugged on his hand. "They love you, Reid, and they just want you to be happy."

He stopped walking and spun me into his arms in the middle of the street. "You make me happy."

He held me tight, and my stomach flipped when he looked at me with those eyes that promised so much more to come.

"I'm glad." I kissed him lightly. Much more than that, I wasn't sure we'd ever make it home. "Because you make me happy, too. And now you're stuck with me."

"There is no one I'd rather be stuck with."

I laughed, but Reid's face remained serious. I loved how intense he was. How grumpy he was for almost everyone and everything except for me.

And Quinn.

I had to admit it made something low in my gut flip over to see the way he had all the time in the world for his niece. It made me think about what a good father he'd be to our kids one day.

Because yes, I wanted that with him. One day. We still had a lot we needed to get through with the inn. I wasn't in a rush anymore. I had my husband. I had my home. And I had no doubt I would have my happily ever after, too.

"What's that look for?" His finger traced my lips.

"What look?"

"That faraway one that means you're thinking about something."

My lips curled up into a smile. "I'm just thinking about us."

"Is that right?" He leaned into me, his breath hot against my mouth.

"Uh-huh."

"All good stuff, I hope."

"So good." My heart raced the way it always did when he looked at me like that. With hunger in his eyes that would never be satiated. I wanted to jump into his arms and show him exactly what that look did to me, but we were still standing in the middle of the street. "Come on." I forced myself to pull away from him before things got indecent in public—again. I grabbed his hand and, before he could protest, tugged him in the direction of home.

Just as I suspected, he didn't resist. But to my surprise, when we finally made it to the front porch, instead of walking me through the front door and pushing me up against the wall to have his way with me, he took my hand and led me to the swing.

"Sit."

"I thought we could—"

"Oh, sweetheart. Make no mistake. I have big plans that involve making you scream out my name over and over again. But first, I would like to sit and have a nice quiet glass of wine with my wife."

I would never get tired of hearing him call me that.

"Will you allow me that?"

How could I say no? "Of course."

He kissed my cheek. "I'll be right back," he said. "I'm going to grab a bottle and a few glasses. Don't go anywhere."

"As if there were anywhere else I'd rather be."

His face softened. He blew me a kiss and disappeared inside.

The stars were out, lighting up the sky. It was one of my favorite things about being in the mountains. You didn't get stars like this in the city. I exhaled slowly and dropped my head back to take them all in.

For the first time in a long time, I felt completely at peace. There were no looming deadlines. No inheritance battles to fight. No fake marriage to untangle.

Not that I was looking to untangle it.

Not even a little bit.

It was something Reid and I hadn't talked about. Not really. We'd just…kept on doing what we were doing. Only it was better now.

"You look like you're thinking about something," Reid said a moment later when he reappeared with a bottle of chilled sauvignon blanc and two glasses.

"Not really." I looked up. "Only how nice this is to be here with you without all the…" I waved a hand in the air, and he laughed. Reid poured us each a glass before joining me on our swing.

I tucked my legs up under me and let Reid push us gently back and forth while we sipped at the wine.

"You know," I said after a few moments. "This is my favorite place in the whole world."

"The inn?"

"No." I shook my head and dropped my head to his shoulder. "This swing. On this porch. At this inn. In this town. With you."

He didn't respond right away, but he didn't need to. I felt it. After a moment, I heard him blow out a breath. "This is my favorite place, too. And you are my favorite person."

I smiled to myself as he sat up and turned so he faced me on the swing. "These last few months have been crazy."

"The craziest." I laughed. "Do you ever think about how this all started with a simple lie?"

He let out a low whistle. "Honestly?" He looked me in the eyes. "All the time."

"You do?"

"Absolutely. And I wouldn't change a thing."

"No?" That surprised me. I knew he didn't like lying to his family.

"No," he said with certainty. "Because if we changed even one little detail, then I don't know if I'd be here with you right now. And I wouldn't trade that for anything."

His fingers trailed down my arm before reaching my hand. He threaded his fingers through mine, his grip warm and sure.

"Avery, being with you is the most real and sure thing I've ever felt in my entire life."

My heart skipped a little, a slow warmth unfurling in my chest. "I feel exactly the same way."

Reid shifted and put his wine down on the porch rail. His free hand came to rest on my knee. "I've been making myself crazy trying to think of the right way to say this, Avery." His finger brushed absentminded circles on my skin, and suddenly he wouldn't look at me. "But I think there's something really important that we need to discuss."

Just like that, my world spun. It was the conversation I'd been worried about. We never discussed it, but maybe he didn't want to be married after all. I knew he loved me, but maybe marriage was too much. If that's what he wanted, I wouldn't fight it, but—

"The truth is," he continued, completely unaware of the tailspin that I'd fallen into, "there's no fancy way to say it."

I swallowed hard, my pulse thudding in my forehead. "Say what?" I was almost afraid to ask.

He exhaled slowly, his gaze locked on mine, steady and sure. "Marry me, Avery."

There was no way I heard him right. "Excuse me, what?"

"Marry me." He was completely serious.

I glanced around nervously. "You do know we already *are* married, right? That was kind of the whole thing…"

His fingers tightened on mine. "Marry me for real, Avery. Not for a will or an inn or for anyone or anything except for you and me." He lifted my hand to his mouth and kissed my knuckles. "Marry me because we *want* to. Marry me because I can't live without you. Marry me because I know you can, but you don't *want* to live without me."

I laughed a little.

"Marry me because we are so good together that we deserve to make this officially official."

"Officially official?" I raised an eyebrow, but the look on his face didn't leave any room for doubt.

"Stay married to me, Avery."

"If this is what I think it is, this is a very strange proposal, Reid." I try to laugh and make light of the moment to give myself time to catch up to what he was saying. "I mean, where's the ring?"

He released my hand long enough to reach into his pocket.

For a moment, my heart stopped. "What is…oh." My hand flew to my mouth as I tried to process exactly what I was seeing. "Is that a…"

"I mean it. Marry me, Avery." Reid slipped from the chair to the floor of the porch and onto one knee. "Stay married to me and let's do it all again. Properly this time. With the wedding you want."

"I don't need a wedding as long as I'm married to you."

"Sweetheart." He held out the ring I still hadn't taken from him. "I didn't say anything about *need*. I said *want*. And

I know you want the wedding. Now, will you or will you not stay married to me, Avery Walker?"

"Yes! Of course. I'd marry you a million times."

With tears in my eyes, I slipped from the swing to my knees in front of Reid, who slid the most beautiful diamond ring onto my left hand before he pulled me to my feet and kissed me and made our engagement official.

Chapter Forty-Three

Reid

AVERY BUZZED WITH NERVOUS ENERGY, and it was damn near impossible to focus on anything else. She bounced from foot to foot and compulsively checked her list.

"Did you—"

"Yes." I nodded. "Put ice in all the buckets for the drinks," I assured her before she could ask the question. "And I also put the drinks in to chill."

She smiled and blew out a breath before lifting the clipboard again.

Gently, I took the list from her hand and set it behind me. "Avery, it's fine." Before she could reach past me to grab it back, I took both her hands in mine. My eye caught on the flash of the diamond on her left hand, and my heart caught the way it always did when I realized that this woman was mine. Really and truly mine.

"It's just that—"

"Avery." I stopped her. "The building is not going to collapse just because you invited half the town inside."

"Not helpful." She shot me a look, but her lips twitched as she tried not to smile. "This is just so important. I don't want to forget anything."

"You didn't." I dropped my teasing tone and pulled her close. "The inn is perfect. You're perfect. And the grand opening is going to be amazing. You've worked your ass off. Relax and enjoy it."

She exhaled and leaned into me for a moment before glancing up at me, a sparkle in her eye. "You just want me to relax so I won't make you give a speech."

I groaned and pressed a kiss to her temple. "You know damn well I'm not giving a speech, sweetheart."

She already asked me three times, and each time I'd given her the same answer. The inn was hers. This day was about her. Sure, I helped and we did a lot of it together, but none of this would be happening if it wasn't for her tenacity and her vision. It was Avery's day.

"I think I can convince you." Her hands slid down my body.

As much as I would have loved to give her the opportunity to try out her methods of persuasion, there was no time. In minutes, the inn would be swarming with family, friends, and neighbors. None of them needed a show.

I caught her hands again and gave her a deep kiss. "I have no doubt I'd love to see you try, sweetheart. But—"

"Is this where the party's at?"

Avery spun at the sound of the voice, and just like that, it was time to celebrate.

. . .

"It looks incredible, Reid." Grayson slapped me on the back and joined me in leaning against the wall, where I'd been watching my wife in her element. It felt like the entire town had come out to see the grand re-opening of the Tamarack Inn and support Avery.

Everywhere I looked, people were laughing, smiling, and admiring the renovations we'd done.

"I can't take any of the credit," I told my brother. "It was all Avery's vision from the very beginning. She knew exactly what she wanted. I was only labor."

He elbowed me in the ribs before lifting his drink to his lips. "We both know that's not true. But I will say, the two of you make a pretty awesome team."

"I won't disagree with that." I let myself smile.

Next to me, Grayson laughed. "I still can't believe it."

"Believe what?" Reluctantly, I looked away from Avery to face my brother. "That we were able to pull it off?"

"Oh no." He scrubbed a hand over his face. "That I can believe. I just can't believe you finally met someone who'd not only put up with your grumpy ass but could also put a smile like that on your face." He laughed again, but I couldn't disagree.

"Gives you hope, does it?" I shot him a look. "I mean, if it can happen for me…"

"Forget it." Grayson blew off my comment the way he always did when someone brought up the subject of women and dating. "It's not happening."

I knew better than to press my twin. He'd been in love once, and it hadn't worked out. We all thought it would take a bit of time for him to get over it and move on, but it had been years since his first love, Harlow, left to pursue her career as a chef. She'd traveled around the world, working with some of the most famous chefs in the business, experiencing amazing things, but Grayson still seemed to be stuck in the past. And it didn't look as if that would change anytime soon.

We stood in easy silence for a few minutes, watching the party around us, when a familiar face broke away from the crowd and headed in our direction.

"I don't mean to interrupt, guys, but you were just the guy I've been looking for." Asher Carlson, along with his fiancé Noa, joined us.

"You're not interrupting anything." I shook Asher's hand and gave Noa a quick hug. It had been a while since I'd seen either of them. Asher and his siblings had grown up with me and my brothers.

Although the Carlson family was widely considered Trickle Creek royalty, with their father Michael known for his business prowess that had ultimately saved the town many years earlier, they were all down-to-earth, genuine people. "Good to see you both. Thanks for coming."

"It's great to have the inn back up and running," Asher said.

"Oh yeah?" I raised an eyebrow. "You're good with a little competition to your condos up at the hill?"

"The way tourism is booming in Trickle Creek, I'm not worried. There's plenty of room for us all to be successful." Asher laughed. "A rising tide and all that."

"All that, indeed." My attitude toward tourists in my town had definitely shifted over the last few months. It had to, considering I would be helping Avery run the inn. It probably wouldn't be good for business if I was openly hostile to the guests.

Besides, Avery helped me see that just because we were opening our doors to tourists didn't mean they'd be taking over our town. Only that we now had the opportunity to share everything we loved with them on our terms.

I still didn't love the fact that people were trying to strip the character from the old homes and "modernize" them, but I'd shifted my approach to potential renovation clients. Instead of getting mad and quitting, giving more work to Danny Davis, I guided them to the more desirable alternative of maintaining the original charm of their properties while updating them. So far, my new approach seemed to be working, and I was all booked up with jobs for the next six months or so.

Avery's influence was rubbing off on me in more ways than one.

"The place really does look incredible," Noa said. "Congratulations."

"Reid won't take any of the credit," Grayson offered. "He's too humble."

"He is," Asher agreed before turning to face me. "But I assume you *will* take credit for that dining room table I saw. In the other room?"

"I will."

About a month earlier, Avery asked me to make the table. *Something solid, something that will last. Like the swing. But somewhere guests can gather and share stories.*

So after the long days working on the inn's endless renovations, I spent my nights at the workshop shaping the thick slabs of oak, sanding every inch until it was perfect. I'd left the edges raw and, right in the middle, I'd carved the same image I had on the swing.

It had turned out better than even I had hoped. Avery cried when she saw the finished product. It was perfect.

"It's beautiful," Noa said. "And so unique."

Asher nodded. "You're very talented, Reid."

"Thank you," I grunted. Accepting compliments did not come naturally to me.

"I'm not sure what your schedule looks like coming up, but we could use some original pieces up at the lodge. Maybe we can meet next week to discuss some commission pieces?"

Commission pieces for the lodge would not only mean a nice little paycheck, but also invaluable exposure for my budding woodworking business. "Absolutely, Asher. That would be fantastic."

"Great." Asher wrapped his arm around Noa. "I'll let you get back to the party. Congratulations on the inn. We'll chat next week."

We said our goodbyes, and when Asher and Noa were out of hearing range, Grayson turned to me with a big grin. "Damn, Reid. Having your work up at the lodge will be huge."

He wasn't wrong.

"It's funny how things work out, huh? And all because I asked you to do me a favor that day at the hardware shop."

"You knew I would say yes."

"Of course I did." He laughed. "But a simple thank-you would do."

"Thank you." I laughed. "But now it's my turn to ask for a favor."

Grayson eyed me. "Oh yeah?"

I nodded seriously. "I need you to be my best man."

My brother's mouth dropped open, and he laughed again. "But you're already—"

"This one's for us." I turned and scanned the crowd, finding my beautiful wife immediately. As if she could sense my eyes on her, she turned and smiled.

Avery lifted her hand in a little wave, and I blew her a kiss.

"Avery deserves a proper wedding," I told Grayson. "And I plan on spending the rest of my life making sure she has anything and everything she wants."

Epilogue

Avery

THE SUN HUNG low on the horizon, casting the most perfect golden glow over the yard of the inn. The air still carried the warmth of the perfect fall day, but a soft breeze whispered through the branches, just cool enough to hint at the season shifting.

We'd been fortunate to have such a warm September, but winter would be upon us before we knew it.

Bright-yellow larch needles drifted down with every breath of wind, covering the ground as well as our guests, like nature's confetti.

It was perfect. The kind of evening that felt like it had been made just for us.

"Avery?"

I looked away from the window to my mom.

"Are you ready?"

"You look beautiful, Mom."

She reached for my hands, a tear in her eye. "Not nearly

as beautiful as you, my girl. Your grandparents…" She inhaled deeply. "I wish they were here to see this. They would be so proud of you."

I swallowed the lump in my throat, refusing to give in to the emotion that had threatened to bubble over all day.

"They are here, Mom."

A tear slipped down her cheek. She wiped at it quickly and forced a smile. "You're right. They are." She squeezed my hands again and held my gaze.

I knew the inn wasn't what my mother had wanted for me and my life. But once she came to visit and she'd met Reid, his family, and all our friends, it hadn't taken long for her to see that Trickle Creek was where I belonged.

"It's time." Carrie's head popped into the bedroom. "Are you ready to live out the ending to your Hallmark movie life?"

I laughed. My best friend had been right after all. It turned out my life was a cheesy, sweet movie with a happy ending.

I turned to give myself one more look in the mirror. My dress was a simple, off-the-shoulder fitted ivory sheath. My hair hung in loose waves, pinned back on one side.

"You look amazing, Avery." Carrie appeared over my shoulder. "Reid won't be able to keep his hands off you." She laughed as my mom swatted her. "Come on. Let's do this."

She handed me a bouquet of sunflowers that had come from the local flower shop and together, we moved to the back door that led out to the yard.

The music started and Carrie, my maid of honor and

best friend, gave me a wink, blew me a kiss, and headed down the steps, to lead our little procession.

Next to me, my mom reached for my hand and squeezed. "I love you, Avery, and I am so incredibly proud of you."

"Thank you, Mom." I gave her a quick hug and then she, too, made her way down the aisle, leaving me alone.

I took a moment to take it all in.

It was exactly how I pictured it. How I'd *wanted* it.

Not a rushed courthouse signature, a technicality wrapped in legal paperwork.

But *this*. This was ours.

And it was perfect.

I smoothed my hands over my dress and tried to calm my racing heart as the music changed.

Everyone stood and turned as I made my way slowly down the steps and up the short, grassy aisle past our guests.

Friends and family who'd all become part of our story.

But I couldn't focus on any of them. Because he was there. Standing in front of the two stunning yellow larch trees, waiting for me.

My husband.

Reid

She was stunning. I was the luckiest man in the world because not only did I get to marry Avery, I got to marry her twice.

Her dress swayed in the soft breeze as the yellow larch

needles drifted down all around us. "You look gorgeous," I told her as she reached me.

Her fingers slid into mine, warm and steady. There was nothing to be nervous about, after all. The hard part was over; this was just for us, and I'd never been so sure about anything in my life. Spending my life with Avery was everything I wanted. Even if I didn't know it a few short months ago.

"You good?" I murmured.

She let out a small breath and smiled. "Never better. You?"

"It's the best day of my life, sweetheart."

That made her laugh. A sweet, soft sound.

Brody, who'd offered to lead the ceremony considering we were already legally married, cleared his throat after a moment. "Are you two ready?"

I nodded but still didn't look away from Avery.

"Friends. Family. We are gathered here today," Brody began, his voice booming over our heads to address our guests, "to celebrate Avery and Reid and their love for each other. And because they didn't invite any of us the first time," he quipped, and the crowd laughed. "But we're all here now," he continued after a moment. "And I think I can speak for all of us when I say that we couldn't be happier for both of them and the love they've found together."

A whoop went up from the crowd. I still didn't look away from my bride, but I did not doubt that it was my youngest brother. I winked at Avery, who laughed again.

"The happy couple have opted to share the vows they've written for each other with us, their closest family and friends to bear witness. Reid? Would you like to go first?"

I inhaled, gathering my strength and nodded. Reluctantly, I released Avery's hand so I could retrieve the piece of paper, where I'd written down a few things I wanted to share.

"Avery, I never planned on getting married. Not like this," I began. "Not at all. Not because I didn't believe in love or happily ever afters, but because I hadn't met you yet. The moment you stormed into my life, all sunshine and determination, everything changed. And somehow, without even trying, you made me want things I'd never even let myself consider before." I looked directly into her eyes. "A home. A future. A forever. And now, I want all of that. With you."

Her eyes shimmered with unshed tears. I swallowed hard before continuing because I, too, could feel emotion welling up.

"You see the best in people, even those who don't deserve it. You find beauty where others only see ruin. And I'll be forever grateful that when you looked at me, you didn't just see the stubborn, grumpy guy who didn't want his life to change—you saw something more. You saw *me*."

Her breath hitched, and a tear slipped down her cheek.

"I can't promise you I'll be perfect, Avery. I'm probably always going to be a little too gruff and a little too set in my ways from time to time. But I do promise to love you." I tucked the paper away—I didn't need it anymore—and reached for her hands. "I promise to wake up every single day and choose you. Over and over again. Just like I'm choosing you now."

She smiled through the tears that streamed unchecked down her cheeks now.

"I love you, Avery."

"I love you, too."

There was no way I could wait a second more. I reached out, wiped the tears from her cheek, and kissed her gently.

A few cheers went up from our guests, and beside me, Brody chuckled before interrupting us.

"I think Avery has a few words she'd like to say as well."

Reluctantly, I pulled back to give her space.

Avery took a breath, steadying herself. Once again, her hands were in mine. Her touch grounded me in the moment. "Okay," she said softly. "My turn.

"Reid, it was only a few months ago that we stood in the courthouse and vowed our commitment to each other. I thought I knew what I was getting myself into. But I couldn't have been more wrong."

A chuckle rumbled in my chest, because we'd both been so wrong.

"I knew when we married, that you would be a reliable partner. Logical, practical, and true. And that you knew how to swing a hammer." She winked. "Sure, you were a grump, but I was pretty sure I could work with that."

Laughter rippled through the crowd.

"But what I didn't realize that first time around was that saying yes to you was saying yes to so much more than a partnership born of necessity. You are the steadiest thing I've ever had in my life. You show up. You stay. Even when it's hard and I try to push you away." She let out a small, shaky laugh. "Even when I insist I don't need help, you know better."

I swallowed back a smile, because *yeah*, that sounded pretty spot on.

"I love you, Reid." Her voice was stronger now, more sure. "For the way you love with actions instead of just words. For the way you know what I need before I do. For the way you see me, even when I try to hide. And most importantly, for the way you're by my side, making me feel safe and watched and like I never have to do it alone ever again."

My heart swelled with love for this woman.

"And that's my promise to you, too," she said, her voice soft but certain. "I promise to share the good times and fill our days with laughter and love. But when the world feels heavy, I vow to stand beside you through it all. Through every hard day, I will be by your side. No matter what happens and what tomorrow brings, I will be by your side. Because I choose you, Reid. Today and every day."

I let out a slow breath and shook my head. "Sweetheart, you're killing me here."

Avery tilted her head up to me, her eyes warm, her lips curled up into a sassy smile. "No, Reid. I'm *keeping* you. Forever."

"Hell yeah, you are."

I kept my eyes locked on hers as I closed the distance between us, cupped her cheeks, and with everything I had in me, kissed my beautiful wife.

Peek in on Reid and Avery the morning after their (for real) wedding night in an exclusive bonus scene, right after this.

Coming next...
Everyone in Trickle Creek is happy about the new brewery Ethan Lyons is opening. Everyone but Delaney, the bookshop owner. Tempers flare and sparks fly when these two clash in More Than Words, next!

Start back at the beginning in Trickle Creek with, Never Let Me Go.

Bonus Scene

Avery

WAKING up in my husband's arms was never going to get old. Especially now that we'd had our proper wedding. I know that some people might have thought it was a little *extra* or totally unnecessary for us to have a whole ceremony followed by a party when we were already legally married.

But I didn't care what any of those people thought. And if they had an opinion about it, they were smart enough to keep it to themselves.

Because our wedding ceremony was perfect.

After our vows, we celebrated with delicious food, more toasts than I could keep track of, and of course as many dances with my new husband as I could get away with.

My feet were throbbing, but I didn't care.

It had been a perfect night.

Almost as perfect as the warm weight of Reid pressed up against me. I wiggled my ass and arched my back into him until the arm he had draped over my waist tightened.

"Good morning, sweetheart." His voice was rough with desire and the remnants of sleep as he woke fully. "Oh yes. It's a very good morning."

"I'd say so." I reached around between us to find his hard dick and squeezed it.

"Mmm." His hand slid down my side and between my legs. "You are perfect," he murmured into my ear before pulling my hair to the side to give him better access to my neck. "And you are so ready for me this morning."

"For you?" Again, I pressed my ass back into him, making him groan. "Always."

Reid growled and before I could brace myself, he somehow managed to roll onto his back and bring me with him so I straddled him.

"Oh, I like this view very much." His hands slid up my body and found my breasts so he could knead and squeeze.

"And I have you just where I want you." I braced myself with my arms, lifting my body just enough so I could lower myself down onto his hard erection.

Matching moans slipped from both of us as I started to roll my hips. It was slow and lazy lovemaking, and after the big night we had, it was absolutely perfect.

Reid's hands were on my hips, slowly guiding my movements. "Have I told you how happy I am that you're my wife?"

I laughed and tossed my hair back. "I've been your wife for months."

"And I was happy all of those months, too."

I laughed again, but my laughter quickly turned to a moan as Reid reached between us and put pressure on my clit.

"I'll spend the rest of my life making you happy, sweetheart."

The pressure built quickly inside me. I squeezed my eyes shut and nodded, unable to focus on anything but the orgasm that was about to crash through me.

"And I think I'll start right now." Reid, sensing how close I was, pressed a little harder. "Come for me, sweetheart."

That's exactly what I did, my husband joining me.

Reid

The only thing better than morning sex was morning sex with my gorgeous wife.

I could have spent my whole day right there in our bed, totally lost to her, making love over and over again. But the footsteps overhead reminded me that we were not alone.

I pulled Avery down into my arms so her head rested on my chest, hoping I could sneak in a few more minutes before our day officially began.

But she'd heard the footsteps, too.

She groaned against my chest. "The problem with owning an inn is that—"

"We have guests?"

She laughed. "We do. And they happen to be family and friends, so we probably shouldn't ignore them too long."

"That's the beauty of it," I countered. "They're not real guests. So they can make their own coffee."

"Ohh, we should have sent them to the Bean Bag for coffee and muffins."

"Is it too late?"

"Yes." She smacked my stomach lightly and pushed off me. "Besides, they're all leaving tomorrow and we'll have the place to ourselves." Avery sat up. Her hair fell in messy waves over her bare shoulders. The warm morning light made her skin glow.

She took my breath away.

"I can't believe it," I said.

"Can't believe that they're all leaving tomorrow or that we'll have the place to ourselves?" She gazed down at me, completely unaware that I was entranced by her beauty.

"No." I reached out and let my finger trail down her arm. "I can't believe how lucky I am that you married me. Twice."

Her face softened and a smile tugged at her lips. "You're so sweet."

"Ha." Laughter rumbled from my chest. "Only for you, Avery. You bring it out in me." I grabbed her arm and tugged her down to me again and kissed her thoroughly. "You bring out all the best parts of me."

The voices outside our door had grown louder as more people woke up and gathered in the kitchen. I knew our time was limited and as much as I wanted to, I wasn't going to be able to keep her in bed all day.

But I at least had a few more minutes before the world intruded, and I planned to make the most of them.

About the Author

Elena Aitken is a USA Today Bestselling Author of more than sixty romance and women's fiction novels. The mother of 'grown up' twins, Elena now lives with her very own mountain man in the heart of the very mountains she writes about. She can often be found with her toes in the lake and a glass of wine in her hand, dreaming up her next book and working on her own happily ever after.

To learn more about Elena:
www.elenaaitken.com
elena@elenaaitken.com